THE CANNIBAL HEART

MARGARET MILLAR

Thorndike Press • **Chivers Press**
Thorndike, Maine USA   Bath, England

This Large Print edition is published by Thorndike Press, USA and by Chivers Press, England.

Published in 2000 in the U.S. by arrangement with Harold Ober Associates Inc.

Published in 2000 in the U.K. by arrangement with The Margaret Millar Charitable Remainder Unitrust u/a 4/12/82.

U.S. Hardcover 0-7862-2335-9 (Mystery Series Edition)
U.K. Hardcover 0-7540-4053-4 (Chivers Large Print)
U.K. Softcover 0-7540-4054-2 (Camden Large Print)

The text of this Large Print edition is unabridged.
Other aspects of the book may vary from the original edition.

Set in 16 pt. Plantin by Minnie B. Raven.

Printed in the United States on permanent paper.

British Library Cataloguing-in-Publication Data available

Library of Congress Cataloging-in-Publication Data

Millar, Margaret.
 The cannibal heart / Margaret Millar.
  p. cm.
 ISBN 0-7862-2335-9 (lg. print : hc : alk. paper)
 1. Large type books. I. Title.
PS3563.I3725 C36   2000
 813'.54—dc21   99-055483

THE CANNIBAL HEART

1

About a hundred yards below the house, to the south, the woods began, and it was here that Luisa said the devils lived. Some of them were shut up in the old well, now gone to salt and useless, and covered with a concrete slab. The others lived in the swimming pool which had been boarded over so they wouldn't escape.

Jessie tried to see the devils by lying on her stomach across the planks and peering through a knot-hole. Inside, there was nothing but blackness and a very faint rustling noise.

"I think I hear something," Jessie said.

"That's them." Luisa hugged her knees and rocked back and forth on the planks with fierce delight. "If you don't quit pesting me and following me around all the time I'll let them loose. I'll tell them to sneak into your room while you're sleeping."

"You wouldn't dare." But the protest was feeble. She knew Luisa would dare. She had, also, an uneasy feeling that if there were any devils in the woods, they belonged to Luisa and would obey her. Luisa wore a veil of mystery. Though she was only fifteen she was already different from other people, and Jessie respected this difference, and despised it, and was a little afraid of it, too. Luisa had wild dark eyes that she could roll up until only the whites were visible, like peeled grapes. She could turn her eyelids inside out by pressing them with her thumb, and when she combed her long black hair in the kitchen, it gave off sparks and made the music, coming from the radio, crackle and splutter. Luisa's family was a little mysterious, too. Her mother, Carmelita, spoke nothing but Spanish — sometimes so fast and loud that Jessie's ears twitched — and Luisa's father, Mr. Roma, had skin as dark and creased as a walnut, and white kinky hair that he kept pressed down tight under a felt hat with two jay feathers stuck in the band.

"Luisa, are you really a Mexican?"

"Half."

"What's the other half?"

"As if you didn't know."

"I don't."

"You must be awfully ignorant for a child nearly nine." Luisa got up, and stretched and yawned with a show of boredom, but

Jessie could tell from her expression that Luisa was offended again. "There's other nasty things in this woods you don't know about, Jessie Banner."

"I don't believe it."

"You don't *live* here like me."

"Now I do. We're going to stay in California until school starts and . . ."

"You're still only a *renter.* I've lived here ever since the house was built, practically before you were born. I know everything about it, and about Mrs. Wakefield, too."

Jessie stirred, and sighed. Luisa was always doing that when she was offended, trapping her into asking questions and then leaving the questions half-answered, or not at all.

She had to ask, anyway; the trap was too tempting. "Who's Mrs. Wakefield?"

"You'll know soon enough. She's coming to get some of her things she left behind. Maybe today, maybe tomorrow. My father had a letter from her. She's going to stay in Billy's room." Luisa put her hands on her hips in exaggerated disdain. "*Now* I suppose you'll want to know who Billy is."

Jessie shook her head and tried to look incurious. "I don't care. Anyway, you're only doing that."

"Doing what, for goodness' sake?"

9

"That. I know lots of Billys at school, anyway. Dozens." This was true. Where she went to school, in New York, Billy was a very ordinary name. She didn't understand how, when it came from Luisa's mouth, it could sound so tantalizing. Spoken by Luisa, it was like one of the words that set off explosive giggling in the cloakrooms or on the playground.

Feigning indifference, she climbed down from the planks and began to pick the dirt out of her scraped knee. In just two weeks she had accumulated more scratches and cuts and bruises than she had in a year at home, and all over her legs and arms there were round red itchy patches that Mr. Roma said were fleabites. Evelyn, her mother, had been quite shocked at this and insisted they must be only mosquito bites, which seemed more respectable. But no, Mr. Roma said, there hadn't been any mosquitos for three years on account of the drought. Only fleas, small as pinheads and just as sharp and strong.

She dug her nails into one of the bites, until pain covered the itching. "What are the nasty things in the woods?"

"You'd be scared out of your skin, Jessie Banner."

"I wouldn't be."

"You mustn't tell a soul, promise on your brother's blood."

"I promise."

"All right then. It's a dead man."

"Right here? Under the — the planks?"

"You really are ignorant. He'd rot under there. You just better go home to your mother and play with your dolls."

"I hate dolls," Jessie lied passionately. "I *never* play with dolls. Where's the dead man?"

"Wouldn't you like to know." Luisa rustled away through the fallen leaves, making a moaning eerie sound in the back of her throat.

"Luisa, wait for me! Luisa?"

But Luisa hid behind a tree and refused to answer to her name.

Jessie looked around carefully at the trees in the hope that she could spot a flutter of Luisa's dress behind one of them, or find evidence of her presence in the sudden squawking of resentful jays, or the scuttling of lizards seeking cover in the brush.

Every tree stood bland, denying Luisa's very existence. In the distance the sea muttered, and from under the planks that covered the dry pool came soft sounds like little unnameable things tittering in the dust below.

She put her hands over her ears and began to run. When she reached the edge of the cliff the muttering of the sea had swollen into a roar that drowned the other noises. She paused, gasping for breath and holding her arm tight against the stitch in her side.

From here she could see a thin gray ribbon of smoke rising from the kitchen chimney, and the barnlike garage on top of which Luisa lived in three rooms with her parents — quite exciting, not like other people who were forced to live in plain houses.

From a distance the big stone house seemed to be growing right out of the cliff like magic. She knew perfectly well it hadn't grown, of course; it had been built, Luisa said, and Mrs. Wakefield had lived there with someone named Billy who wasn't like the Billy Jessie knew at school.

She stooped and peered over the edge of the cliff so she could watch the shiny black cormorants swoop out from their nests in the holes of the cliff side and dive for fish. But she suddenly detested the big ravenous birds; and everything — the sea and the gray house, the fleabites on her legs and the woods pressing on her heels — seemed alien and monstrous. She wished she were back at home, walking in Central Park with one of her aunts, or riding jam-packed on the subway where there were so many people so very much alive that she couldn't imagine dead ones. Her face squeezed up, as if it might, without asking her permission, begin to cry. She herself never cried, especially not if there was a chance that Luisa might be spying on her.

She rose and pushed her straight yellow hair back off her forehead. She began walking toward the house, whistling blithely and as loud as she could, in case Luisa was within earshot.

2

Evelyn's face was needled with dust and her brown hair blowing against her neck felt as dry and stiff as straw.

"Next time you should wear a hat," Mr. Roma said. "Mrs. Wakefield always wore a hat when she drove into town, a straw hat with a brim. She had a very fair complexion."

He turned out to avoid a hole in the road, and the boxes of groceries slid across the back seat and the milk cans, packed in ice, rattled and gurgled.

"On this road," he said, "it is like the desert. You must keep covered up for protection."

In spite of the heat he wore a heavy plaid wool jacket buttoned to the neck, and a gray fedora jammed well down on his head so that only a little of his white hair showed at the back of his neck. He had eyes like brown plush, and a full sensitive mouth that quivered when he was moved to emotion; but it was chiefly the prematurely white hair that gave Mr. Roma his air of distinction. To

Evelyn he looked like an English colonel charred by a tropic sun. She was surprised when he told her he was a mulatto.

"Perhaps," Mr. Roma said, "next Saturday I could go alone and do the shopping."

"Oh, no. I really enjoy shopping."

"It's not much of a town to buy things in," he said in a half-deprecating, half-hopeful tone. Marsalupe was the only town he knew very well, and while he realized its limitations, he wanted other people to approve of it, especially strangers from the East. "There are no delicacies."

"I don't like delicacies much," Evelyn said with a faint smile.

"You can always order things from Los Angeles. Mrs. Wakefield did that sometimes. Once, hearts of palm in a can. Mr. Wakefield had a sudden craving for it. It's a great delicacy. Compared to hearts of palm, caviar is as common as dirt." After a time he added, "From this curve it's only a mile and a half. Already you can smell the sea."

Evelyn couldn't smell the sea, though she sniffed hard to oblige Mr. Roma, who always spoke as if he had a controlling interest in the sea as well as in the house built on the cliff above it.

"Don't you smell it, Mrs. Banner?"

"Well, not quite. It's not like a smell, exactly. It's more like a *feeling* against my skin."

"I smell it very clearly."

"There, I think I do now. Yes, I'm sure of it."

Evelyn didn't like anyone to be disappointed. It was this characteristic that led some of her friends into thinking she was weak-willed; and once Mark, in a fit of temper, had told her she was wispy, that she had a wispy personality and a wispy mind. Sometimes, especially when she first got up in the morning and wasn't quite awake, she felt wispy, like a floating, detached piece of fog. But once she'd washed the sleep from her eyes she saw herself quite distinctly as a person of substance, and by the time she went into the adjoining bedroom to help Jessie dress, she felt as clear and sharp and hard as a diamond.

The fact remained that at thirty-two Evelyn was, as she always had been, a very practical creature. It was often practical to make people, like Mark or Mr. Roma, feel good; and so she smelled the sea and told Mr. Roma that she felt refreshed already.

Mr. Roma was very pleased to have the salubrious qualities of his ocean recognized, and he rounded the next curve with such

16

sweeping grace that Evelyn clutched at the door with both hands to balance and the groceries and the milk cans and the books for Mark slid in noisy unison to the other side of the jeep.

For the past eight years Mr. Roma had been making his Saturday trips to Marsalupe for supplies. It was only a matter of nine miles, but few people used the road and it was left in bad repair. During the wet season Mrs. Wakefield's heavy Lincoln used to sink to its hub caps in mud, and during the dry season the road was dusty and full of holes, and there was about a mile of slide area where unexpected boulders brushed the old Lincoln's tires and tortured its ageing springs. After the war Mrs. Wakefield bought a second-hand jeep which raced along the road like a tireless and indestructible child. When Mrs. Wakefield departed suddenly, over a year ago, she left the jeep with Mr. Roma.

Every month Mr. Roma received a check from Mrs. Wakefield's bank, to cover his salary and necessary repairs for the house. Together, he and Carmelita had kept the place ready for occupancy, expecting that at any time Mrs. Wakefield would send word that she and Billy were coming home. But the only news he had of her were two letters, the first from Billy's nurse.

"Dear Mr. Roma: Mrs. Wakefield wrote and asked me to put the house in the hands of a real-estate agent here in San Diego. She wants you to stay on until a sale is made. This may not be for a long time because of the drought affecting the water supply and also because the house is quite out of the way and most people have to go out and scrounge for a living just like me! Mrs. Wakefield and Billy returned from Port-au-Prince three months ago but set out again immediately on a cruise down the coast. (By a funny coincidence they went on the *Eleutheria*, which is, I recall, one of the last ships poor Mr. Wakefield helped to design. Life is odd, isn't it?) My best wishes to yourself and Carmelita, and tell Luisa I wish her all kinds of luck on her exams.

Norma Lewis.

P. S. I've just talked to the real-estate man and he says there's not a *chance of* selling the house until something is done about the water situation — I guess he means rain. Meanwhile he has an opportunity to rent it furnished, for the

18

summer only, to some people from New York, a man and wife and a child of school age. The man has some connection with publishing books, and he's got good bank references. He's willing to pay $2000 up to September 15th (including you and Carmelita, of course). I think it's a good offer, considering the disadvantages of the place. Anyway I said, go ahead. I guess it'll be all right, though I do think it would be nicer if Mrs. Wakefield kept in closer touch with me!

N. L."

A week after the Banners had moved in, the second letter arrived. It was an abrupt little note from Mrs. Wakefield herself, telling Mr. Roma that he might expect her within a week or two, and that she wanted to "straighten out a few things."

"One more hill," Mr. Roma said, shifting into second. "Maybe you would care to stop and see the view?"

"For a minute."

"Mrs. Wakefield's been all over, in nearly all the countries, and she says right here is the most wonderful view in the world."

Evelyn smiled again. She couldn't help being amused by Mr. Roma's soft intensity,

19

his air of innocent earnestness. "Perhaps it's because this is her home, she has a sentimental attachment."

Mr. Roma gave her a sharp glance. "She has no such attachment."

"She must be unusual then."

"Unusual, oh, yes. She's a real — a real *gentlewoman*." He handled the word awkwardly, as if he was aware that it was obsolete but could find no newer word to take its place.

"Is she pretty?"

"Some people think so. It is a matter of opinion. She has fine eyes and hair — red hair, quite dark."

He stopped the jeep at the top of the hill. The road curved down below them through a grove of giant eucalyptus trees. Beyond the trees the sea shone blue and silver, with the cliffs zigzagging along its shore. As far as the eye could see, the cliffs stretched, a wilderness of stone, with here and there part of a house visible, or a tendril of rising smoke that implied a house with people living in it. There were no people to be seen, though — no movement at all except the sea. From such a height even the sea looked sluggish, and the breakers crawled languidly along the beach.

"There's an island out there," Mr. Roma

said, pointing. "Twenty miles or so."

"I can't see it."

"Not today — there is a slight haze — but on some days you can see it quite clearly."

She thought instantly of Jessie, how eager she would be to see the island and explore.

"It would be fun to go over there some time, rent a cruiser in Marsalupe . . ."

"There's no place to land."

"How do people live there?"

"No one does. There are no people on the island because there is no water."

"Water," Evelyn repeated. She had never before in her life thought of water except as something that came obligingly, hot or cold, from a tap. But out here it was all she heard about, and everywhere she looked she saw reminders: the disconnected showers; the big tub under the kitchen sink where Carmelita saved the rinse water to use later on the vegetable garden, soap and all; the bricked-in flower beds, empty and baked into clay by the incessant sun, and the lawn that was so dry and crisp it crackled under one's feet. *When the rains start,* people said, or, *When the dry season is over.* They measured time in cups and gallons.

When they passed the grove of eucalyptus trees the house itself came into view. It was a comfortable house, built sturdily and economically of adobe brick and native stone. But to Evelyn the place had a curious air of unreality, as if the people who had lived there had formed a small compact group independent of the outside world, the daily newspaper, the radio, the postman. In actual fact, the newspaper came (a day or two late), the mail was delivered, and there was a Capehart in the living room. But still the impression of isolation so strong that Evelyn hesitated before turning on the radio, and once it was turned on she soon lost interest. "We're becoming a couple of lotus eaters," Mark had said, and it was true that, day by day, they were being absorbed by the house and the sea and the woods. Any other life seemed more and more remote.

The main rooms of the house faced the sea, but at the back there was a huge kitchen where Carmelita did the cooking and the Romas ate all their meals and spent most of their leisure time. To the north was the L-wing, two rooms and bath, now unoccupied. This wing was subtly different from the rest of the house, but it wasn't until now, when Mr. Roma parked the jeep outside the kitchen door, that Evelyn realized why.

"That's funny," she said. "I didn't notice it before."

"What?"

"The windows remind me of a jail."

Mr. Roma smiled and said they did, at that, though he volunteered no explanation of the fine wire mesh that unobtrusively covered the windows.

Evelyn managed to look wispy but obstinate. "Why would anyone put windows like that in a house?"

"Because of Billy. Mrs. Wakefield was afraid that Billy might break a window and hurt himself."

"She must be one of these over-protective mothers."

"Must be." Mr. Roma honked the horn to summon Carmelita to help carry in the groceries.

"I'll take some of the things in," Evelyn said.

"Oh, no, thank you. Carmelita always helps. Carmelita is very strong."

In response to the horn, Carmelita came out onto the back porch. She was a fat stubborn woman with fierce dark eyes, like Luisa's. She wore loose huaraches on her feet, and her head was wrapped in a red silk scarf. Luisa insisted that her mother be stylish, and she had taught her how to do her hair up in pin curls. Carmelita wanted to please, and so she did her hair up in bobby pins once a week and tied a scarf around it.

23

There, for the rest of the week the scarf and the bobby pins remained intact. It was Camelita's way of obliging Luisa without taking too much trouble about it. No one could say she was not stylish, with all her pin curls.

In spite of her weight Carmelita had a proud willowy walk, and she carried her head high, in great disdain. The truth was that she was frightened of people who couldn't speak her language; her neck got quite stiff with fright sometimes, but she never told anyone.

"Carmelita is as strong as a horse," Mr. Roma said with pride. "Aren't you? Eh?"

Carmelita flashed him a brief impatient smile, and, lifting two of the milk cans, strode back into the kitchen. Mr. Roma followed her in with the larger box of groceries. While Evelyn picked up the books from the back seat, she could hear the two of them talking in staccato Spanish. A minute later Mr. Roma came out again. He had put on his spectacles, the pair that Carmelita had chosen herself in the dollar store in Marsalupe.

He looked at Evelyn over the top of the spectacles. "I have had a letter. Mrs. Wakefield is coming today or tomorrow."

"That's fine."

"She will not bother you. She said to tell you that."

"We'll be glad to have her," Evelyn said truthfully. "Is she bringing her little boy with her?"

"No" — Mr. Roma took off his hat and rubbed the deep red wound across his forehead where the hat had been squeezed down tight to foil the wind — "the little boy is dead."

Later, when everything was put away, the paper bags folded, and the pieces of string wound on a twist of paper to save for a rainy day, Mr. Roma settled down in the platform rocker beside the kitchen window and read the letter aloud, translating to Carmelita as he went along.

It was dated Monday, June 14, three days earlier than the postmark, as if Mrs. Wakefield had hesitated about sending it once it was written.

"Dear Mr. Roma: I thought I'd better enlarge on my previous note. When I returned and found Mr. Hawkins had rented the house, I was rather upset. But what's done is done, and I guess it's just as well to get some income out of it while I'm waiting to sell. It distresses me to think that so much of my stuff should be lying around the house in the way of these people who probably have their own pictures and drapes, etc., to use . . .

("They haven't," Carmelita said shortly. "They've got nothing but books. Books and clothes."
"She doesn't know that.")

". . . I am driving up on Saturday or Sunday. Mr. Hawkins tells me I should make my own inventory of the contents of the house. It seems like an awful bother, but I must come, in any case, to pick up some of the very personal things I left behind, the trunk of toys and clothes in Billy's room, and the camellia tree in the tub (if it's still alive after this terrible year), and things like my records, and the music in the piano bench. . . ."

("All marches," Carmelita said. "All fast quick marches."
Mr. Roma nodded. He knew by heart all the marches that Mrs. Wakefield had played on the piano. She always played them good and loud, while Billy sat on the floor beside her, moving head and arms in a queer helpless way as if he wanted to keep time.)

". . . This inventory business may take me a few days, or perhaps a week. If these people don't mind me sleeping in Billy's old room, I can eat my meals with you and Carmelita. It will be good to see you both again, though painful, too. We've been through so much together. Perhaps all deep friendships have been watered by tears, ours more than most — John's and yours and Carmelita's — Billy was the only one of us who never cried . . ."

(Carmelita's lower lip began to tremble and she turned and wiped her eyes with the hem of her apron.)

". . . I didn't intend to tell you this in my letter, but I suppose it makes no difference how I tell it. Billy is dead. He died three weeks ago quite suddenly. He was nine years and twenty-eight days old. I know he is in better hands than mine.

Janet Wakefield."

For a long time Mr. Roma sat with the letter in his hand staring out of the window, while Carmelita wept into her apron and shuffled back and forth across the kitchen, up and down its length.

"I had to burn the camellia, there was nothing left of it but sticks," Mr. Roma said at last. "She will be disappointed."

The camellia had died, not suddenly, but with a slow sure finality. The tired buds dropped, shriveled before they opened, and the leaves turned black and fell, one by one.

3

It was one of Jessie's new characteristics that when she was frightened she no longer ran to her mother or father to be comforted, she comforted herself. If she was badly frightened she shut herself up in her room and sobbed into her pillow. If she was only half-frightened she went into her mother's room and dressed up in her mother's clothes. Traces of tears were covered up with rouge, and over her own small mouth she painted a voluptuous and sophisticated pair of lips.

When Evelyn went upstairs she found her parading in the hall, wearing a pink satin nightgown and green high-heeled sandals.

"That's my best nightgown," Evelyn said.

"I'm not hurting it."

"It's dragging on the floor. The hem is dirty already. See?"

"It's good clean dirt," Jessie protested. "Not like tar or paint or anything."

"Well, I think you'd better change anyway, and wash your face while you're at it."

"But I haven't even had time to see myself yet. I want to see if I look eighteen."

"Well, come on then. We'll both see."

She led the way into Jessie's room, with Jessie, voluntarily crippled by the high heels, flopping and shuffling along behind her.

In the door of Jessie's closet was a full-length mirror.

"Do I look eighteen?"

"Not quite."

"Seventeen?"

"Just about seventeen, I guess."

"Older than Luisa anyway," Jessie said in bitter triumph.

She held up her arms while Evelyn pulled off the satin nightgown, revealing the soiled cotton playsuit underneath.

Jessie began to brush the twigs out of her hair. All her movements were quick and vigorous, like Mark's, and she was beginning to look more like Mark every day. In the past year her face had lost its round babyish contours and her nose seemed larger. It was no longer an indeterminate button, it had a definite shape and character, like Mark's nose in miniature.

"When I grow up," Jessie said thoughtfully, "I'm going to boss Luisa around and tell her lies."

"We won't be here when you're grown-up."

"I can always come back. I'll get married and make my husband bring me back."

Evelyn smiled, a little anxiously. "Why should you want to tell lies to anyone?"

"Because."

Jessie put down the brush and began to rub off her lipstick with a piece of tissue. She didn't rub very hard. There was always the faint chance that her mother would let her leave a trace of it on. Jessie didn't know why this large mature mouth was important to her, but it was. She felt better with it on, more capable of dealing with Luisa and the secrets in the woods.

"Do you believe in devils?"

Evelyn shook her head briskly. "Of course not."

"Neither do I," Jessie said, without conviction.

"You'd better use some soap. Who told you about devils?"

"No one."

"Was it Luisa?"

Mute and stubborn, Jessie fixed her gaze on a fly sitting on the mirror cleaning its legs.

"You didn't answer my question, Jessie."

"You ask so many questions. I can't answer everything. I'm not a genius."

Evelyn let out a sigh of exasperation. "You don't have to be a genius to answer yes or no."

Jessie moved her head so that the fly on the mirror seemed to be sitting interestingly on her left eye. Then she tried the fly on her nose and her right eye and the middle of her mouth.

"You're getting so obstinate," Evelyn said. "I can't understand it. If Luisa frightened you I want to know about it, so I can make her stop. After all, she's only fifteen, she's got very little more sense than you have."

Mark came in from the hall. He had been reading in the sun and he wore his khaki shorts and a towel around his shoulders where the skin was beginning to peel. He was a tall, decisive man, with handsome but slightly irregular features, and an air of controlled impatience. Though he was thirty-eight, he looked younger, partly because he wore a crew-cut, a reminder of the days he'd spent in the Navy during the war.

"What's up now?" he said. "Are you two girls arguing again?"

Jessie gave him a brief cold glance. She didn't like her father to go around the house in shorts because he had hair on his chest which looked silky but felt like wire. To Jessie this hair was rather mysterious and secret and should be kept covered up, except when her father went in swimming. Luisa said that lots of men had hair on their chests,

32

and that it was a sign. She wouldn't tell Jessie what it was a sign of, but Jessie knew from Luisa's sudden gust of giggling that it was something little girls weren't supposed to discuss.

"I wasn't arguing," she said with a scowl. "I was just keeping a secret."

"Lord, another one." Mark rubbed his eyes and yawned. "Get the books, Evelyn?"

"Some. Not the ones you asked for. Marsalupe is hardly the most literate metropolis west of the Mississippi. You'll save time by wiring for them."

Still scowling, Jessie explored with her teeth the hangnail on her right thumb. She had been aware for some time now that as soon as her father came into the room there was a subtle shift of interest, away from herself. It seemed that this shift was Evelyn's fault; when Mark was around Evelyn focused her eyes on him, steadily and intensely, as if he had just come back from a long journey and was leaving again at any moment. Jessie, left with mere sidelong glances, felt neglected. To draw Evelyn's eyes back to herself again, she kicked the leg of the vanity, not too hard.

"Stop that," Evelyn said. "Honestly, angel, I've *told* you — the furniture isn't ours."

"It's Luisa's, so I don't care."

"No, it's not Luisa's, either. Mark, you tell her."

"Tell her what?"

"Not to kick the furniture."

"O.K. Do not kick the furniture," Mark said obligingly. "Kick Luisa, if you have to kick."

"Mark, for heaven's sake, don't say things like that to her."

"Damn it, I mean it. That girl's driving me loco. She haunts me, she creeps out from behind trees, she . . ."

"Maybe she has a crush on you."

"I'm as old as her father."

"Even so."

The shift of attention again; the invisible string that bound Mark and Evelyn, that Jessie could tangle but not break.

"She'd kick me back," Jessie said, feeling around for the string, tugging at it subtly. "Hard, too. Oh, I just hate Luisa!"

"Why?" Mark asked.

"I can't tell. Luisa said not to tell."

"Come on, baby."

Jessie was silent a moment. "She said there were devils in the woods. Under the boards of the swimming pool."

Mark's quick frown was in Evelyn's direction. "That girl's getting to be a damned nuisance. You'll have to talk to her."

"I already have."

"Then you weren't firm enough."

"I tried to be," Evelyn said, looking baffled. She hadn't been firm, of course, but she had tried, several times and at several different levels, to make friends with Luisa. But the girl was unresponsive and Evelyn had found it impossible to talk to her. Sometimes, racing down to the beach behind Jessie to dig for clams at low tide, Luisa seemed to be a child, as wild and free as the cormorants that lived on the face of the cliff. But when she was doing her tasks, dusting or helping her mother in the kitchen, or collecting the eggs from the chicken pen, she looked as old and shrewd as Carmelita herself. Luisa's life seemed to be a dance before mirrors, all of which were more or less distorted. No one could see the real Luisa through these mirrors, and Luisa herself could not see out.

"You didn't see any devils, did you?" Evelyn said.

"I heard them."

"What nonsense! Come with Mark and me and we'll show you what nonsense it is."

"I'd rather — stay here." She saw that her mother had turned quite pale, so that the freckles on the bridge of her nose and across her cheekbones stood out like brown crumbs on a white tablecloth.

"Now listen, Jessie. Do you want to know the real reason why the pool was boarded up? It was because the lady who used to live here was afraid her little boy might fall in. See, they couldn't spare any water to put in the pool, and you can take a pretty bad tumble into a dry swimming pool."

"What was the little boy's name?"

"Billy. Billy Wakefield."

Jessie nodded. Now that the little boy had such a real-sounding name, it was very possible that he was a real boy, not a once-there-was boy. This real boy was given to falling from places and into places, just like Jessie herself, so the story about the swimming pool sounded quite plausible.

"I never believed there were devils," she said contemptuously. "I ran away for fun to scare Luisa."

Mark raised his thick straight eyebrows in a half-amused way. "Even so, I think we'll settle this business once and for all. Come on, Jess. We'll go and get Luisa and investigate the pool."

"She won't come."

"She'll come if I have to drag her by the hair."

Jessie giggled at this delightful vision —

36

Luisa being dragged through the woods by her long crackly hair, screaming piteously. Luisa bereft of her magic powers. Luisa unbewitched, cut down to girl-size again.

Walking down the steps between her father and her mother, Jessie felt wonderfully brave.

"I forgot to tell you, Jess," Mark said. "We're having company today or tomorrow."

"Company with children?"

"No children, no. It's a grown-up lady called Mrs. Wakefield."

"That's the little boy's name. Why isn't she going to bring him with her?"

"I don't know," Mark said, after a slight hesitation.

Jessie let out a squeal of anticipation.

Company, even if it was only another grown-up lady, was always exciting. It meant someone new to talk to without interruption, and a new pair of eyes to marvel at her hoard of treasures — the doll igloo she was making out of abalone shells, her new friend, James the gander who could make fearful noises, the double swing Mr. Roma had hung from the pepper tree, and, best of all, the baby starfish she had found yesterday in a tide pool. The starfish was no bigger than a silver dollar, and Jessie kept it in a bowl of sea water in her room and fed it everything she could think of that a starfish might like.

"When is she coming?"

"We don't know exactly."

"I'll show her my starfish and I'll take her down to see . . ."

"Well, don't make a nuisance of yourself," Mark said, with a little warning glance. "And don't talk her head off. She's — not feeling very well."

"Has she got nerves like you?"

"That's right."

They found Luisa in a corner of the kitchen reading a movie magazine and sucking an orange. She kept her gaze fixed on the magazine, deliberately ignoring their presence, until Mark spoke:

"We're going to take a little walk in the wood. We'd like you to come along."

Luisa's eyes narrowed with suspicion, and she shook her head, with the orange still fastened to her mouth like a huge leech.

"I'd like to see these ghosts or devils of yours, Luisa."

Luisa opened her mouth and the orange dropped into her lap. "I didn't do a thing to her," she said, with a black look at Jessie. "I didn't do a single thing."

"Come along, anyway."

They walked in single file out the door.

James the gander waddled over from his usual place beneath the magnolia tree. No one knew for certain why he preferred this spot, though Mr. Roma had suggested that it was because the fresh-fallen magnolia petals looked like huge snowy goose-eggs.

He advanced on them, hissing in a half-friendly, half-warning manner. James' origin was uncertain; he had simply appeared one day, and stayed. He was very old now, and his one eye had clouded and his temper was uncertain, but he still felt it was his duty to patrol the yard, and keep things in order. Though he actually despised people, he sometimes needed them, in the absence of geese or other ganders. At night, when he had a spell of loneliness, he rapped his bill against the lighted windows, or scraped it up and down the screen door of the kitchen, coaxing for a little companionship, however objectionable it might be. It was difficult to be fond of James because of his haughty contempt for the human race, but it was equally difficult to dislike him.

Hissing, he followed them as far as the garage, then circled back again to the magnolia tree with cumbersome dignity.

"Here, James," Jessie called. "Come on, James." The gander snorted, and shuffled round and round among the fallen petals of the magnolia.

The beginning of the path that led to the woods was made of flagstones, bordered on the left with scraggly pelargoniums, and on the sea side a cypress hedge to break the wind. The cypress was dying from the drought, and when the wind touched it, it mourned and dropped its needles like tears. Further on, where the flagstones ended, the path was crackly with oak leaves that stung Jessie's bare feet.

At the pepper tree where Mr. Roma had hung Jessie's swing, the path curved abruptly to the left, past a wide barranca filled with scrub oak, and huge boulders where the lizards sunned themselves at noon. Over the barranca there was a bridge made of planks and wire cable, but no one knew who had built it, or how old it was and how safe. When the wind blew, the bridge rocked and squeaked, and the only ones who ever used it were the jays and the mocking birds who came to sing and quarrel and splatter their droppings, and the termites who tunnelled through the planks, leaving behind tiny pellets of wood.

With Jessie in the lead, they scrambled down over the boulders and up on the other side into a grove of eucalyptus and juniper trees. In a clearing in the middle of the grove was the small swimming pool, neatly covered with planks nailed together at the ends. It looked like a raised little dance floor, and this was precisely what Jessie had used it for until today.

"Well, *I* don't see any devils," Mark said, with exaggerated surprise.

"I just *told* her that," Luisa muttered.

"Why?"

"I had to tell her something. She's always following me. No matter where I go she follows me. I've got a life of my own to live." She glanced at Mark out of the corner of her eye. "Besides, she wanted to take the boards off. She got a hammer out of the garage."

"I wanted it to be a wading-pool," Jessie said anxiously. "In case it rains."

"The boards are supposed to stay on. Mrs. Wakefield said so. She put them on herself."

Mark went over and tried to loosen one of the planks but it wouldn't budge. "She did a good enough job. It seems a funny spot to build a pool in the first place."

"Mr. Wakefield liked privacy," Luisa said. "He didn't like anyone else around." The mention of Mr. Wakefield seemed to make her uneasy. She glanced over her shoulder and added in a burst, "Can I go now? I'm supposed to be watching the beans."

"It's getting chilly," Evelyn said. "We might as well all go, if Jessie is satisfied. You're not frightened any more, are you, Jessie?"

"No." Jessie stared grimly down at her big toe where two ants were rather ticklishly playing follow the leader. Mr. Roma said all the ants were searching for water, which was why they often invaded the kitchen and the downstairs bathroom. Thoughtfully, Jessie spit on the ground, and then with her forefinger she eased the thirsty ants off her big toe so they could locate the spit. "I was never frightened *a bit*."

She raised her head and saw Luisa's faint sneer, and the amused skeptical glances exchanged by her parents. Their disbelief astounded her, and when she spoke again her voice trembled with intensity:

"I'll stay here and prove it. You just watch me!"

Ducking past her mother she leaped up on the planks and began stamping her feet and shouting challenges.

"Leave her alone," Mark said. "She has to work out her own problems."

When they reached the house again they could still hear Jessie's faint scornful chant mingling with the rise and fall of the sea and the sighing of the cypress — *I'm the king of the castle and you're the dirty rascals.*

Mark closed the windows of the living room so he couldn't hear it. But it wouldn't be shut out. It kept beating rhythmically inside his head and the pulse in his temple throbbed in time to it.

He glanced across the room at Evelyn, sitting, mute and placid as a china doll, in the wing chair by the window. For a moment he felt a savage resentment against her placidity; it ripped through his body and out again, like an electric current. It seemed to Mark that she lived entirely on and off the surface; her strongest emotions were affection, dislike, anger. She enjoyed weeping at movies, and she was always careful to bring her own handkerchief. It had been one of the little things about her that amused him when they were first married, and it still did, if he was in the right mood. But the right moods were becoming more infrequent.

"Did you ever sing that when you were a kid?" he said.

"I suppose. I can't remember."

"You must have been a funny kid. Did you ever have anything to say for yourself?"

"I'll go up and get your sweater."

"No, sit down. I don't need it."

"I hope we're not going to quarrel," Evelyn said.

"Why should we?"

"I don't know, but it seems that every time Jessie has a problem, it always turns into *our* problem, into an argument between you and me."

"I don't feel like arguing," Mark said. "Do you?"

"Then why start something?"

"I wasn't," she said patiently. "I was only pointing out what's happened so often, so it wouldn't happen again, so we'd be on guard."

"It sounds more as if you meant *en garde*."

"No."

"You're not jealous, are you?" Mark said. "There's no one around here to be jealous of except Luisa, and she's a little on the young side."

"Don't be silly. You know I've only been jealous once in my whole life."

"By God," he said bitterly. "You'd think I'd have lived that Patty business down by now."

"Patty's a ridiculous name for a woman her age. Patty. It sounds more like a cocker spaniel, or one of those hounds with awfully long ears."

"A basset."

"That's it." She crossed the room and put her arms around his neck and clung there. She was so small and light he barely felt her weight. "We *mustn't* quarrel, darling!"

"We're not quarreling."

"Especially with that woman coming, and Jessie in one of her moods."

He bent down and kissed her lightly on the forehead, but he felt that little surge of rebellion pass through him again. Whether there had been a quarrel or not, she had won.

He wanted suddenly, like Jessie, to stand up his feet and shout at the top of his lungs, *I'm the king of the castle.*

4

When her voice got tired Jessie sat down on the lid of the well and gently bit at the hangnail on her right thumb. The hangnail was the worst she'd ever had and she had an idea that she might leave it on to show to the visitor. Since Carmelita had partly charmed her wart away with funny noises and hot castoroil, Jessie had no physical distinction left except the hangnail.

Jessie took her thumb away from her mouth and examined the remains of the charmed wart on the joint of her forefinger. Though her parents said that no one could charm things away, Jessie could see the evidence for herself — the wart was nearly gone. She wondered how Carmelita got this awful power of diminishing things, and whether she could use it on animals or people, to turn whales into minnows, or Jessie herself into a storybook doll.

"I could charm things," she whispered to herself. "Carmelita can teach me and when I go back to school I'll charm everyone's diseases."

It was impossible to sit still on such an exhilarating thought. She jumped up laughing and spread her arms wide. It was wonderful to be herself, Jessie, powerful and unafraid, and with company coming. Dancing on her toes she started off down the path for home while the little lizards darted out of the way of her flying feet.

Just before she came to the curve in the path she stopped for breath, and it was then that she heard clearly, above all the other little noises in the woods, a new noise that she didn't recognize.

She crouched down behind a boulder and listened. The rhythmic squeaking continued, and the harder she listened the more familiar it seemed. Yet it was oddly out of place. No one used the swing in the pepper tree except Jessie, herself, and, very rarely, Luisa; but the sound was now unmistakable, the crunch-squeak of rope against bark.

She called out, "Luisa?" and her voice sounded very high and thin, as if Carmelita had charmed most of it away.

There was no answer from Luisa. Jessie had expected none. Even if Luisa had heard her she knew Luisa wouldn't answer anyway because she was mad. Luisa's madness might last forever, and this thought made Jessie feel quite desperate and reckless.

There was no use trying to appease Luisa, so she might as well do her best to scare her out of her skin.

Cautiously she approached the curve of the path, keeping close behind tree trunks and boulders, and crawling on her hands and knees when she had to cross an open space.

In spite of all her care she couldn't prevent the leaves and twigs from crackling under her weight, and by the time she reached the place where she could see the swing, the squeaking noise had stopped. Crouched behind an oak tree, ready to pounce, she waited for the noise to begin again, so that she could catch Luisa unaware and dreaming.

She waited for a long time, until her one foot went to sleep and she had to wake it by slapping and pinching. When she finally gave up her vigil and stepped out from behind the tree she saw that there was no one on the swing at all, though it was still moving in the wind.

Furious at being tricked and missing her prey, she shouted feebly, "You're a stinker! If you hide on me I'm going to tell!"

She saw then, moving through the trees like two giant gaudy birds, Mr. Roma in his plaid shirt, and a woman who wore a yellow dress and had a blaze of dark red hair.

48

★ ★ ★

"It's the little girl, Jessie," Mr. Roma said. "She likes to make noises. It is good for her lungs."

Mrs. Wakefield smiled faintly. Her eyes didn't change but the lines around her mouth deepened. "It must be funny to have a child around again."

"It is very lively."

"Lively, yes." She turned away, blinking. "They are nice people, are they?"

"Yes, I think so," Mr. Roma said gently. "Mr. Banner is restless, he is lonely maybe, but not the lady or the little girl."

Mrs. Wakefield paused beside an acacia tree and touched it with her hand as if it were an old friend. The acacia had never been pruned and its gray fringed leaves drooped to the earth. The yellow blossoms, like tiny balls of chenille, had browned and withered.

"Nearly everything has died but the trees," Mrs. Wakefield said. "It pays to have deep roots."

Kneeling down on the carpet of withered blossoms she began to brush them away with her hand.

"I'll do it," he protested. "Here. Look. I have my handkerchief."

"No. How old is the little girl?"

49

"Nearly nine. She will be nine next month."

"Almost as old as Billy. You'll have to have a birthday party for her."

"Oh, yes."

"Tell me the date so I can think of it when I'm gone."

"The eighteenth of July."

She repeated the date aloud. "It will be a nice thing to think of, a little girl's birthday party."

Mr. Roma knew she would remember; the very first thing in the morning on July the eighteenth, she would think of Jessie's birthday party. He wanted to make the picture real for her so that she would be, in a sense, at the party herself.

"Carmelita will bake an angel's food cake," he said seriously, "with pink icing and nine pink candles. Inside the cake will be a ten-cent piece and a little silver horseshoe . . ."

"And a wedding-ring. Perhaps Luisa will get the wedding-ring. She'd like that."

"Yes, the cake will be filled with many things," Mr. Roma said.

In the space which he had cleared of blossoms was a small square stone. Mr. Roma had placed it in the ground himself and he had no need to look at the words it bore:

John Harris Wakefield, 1898-1947, God Rest His Soul.

He turned his eyes away, toward the sea glimmering like a blue light beyond the gray leaves of the acacia. He didn't want to see Mrs. Wakefield's silent, tearless grief. He knew she would not weep, she had gone dry like an old well. The dryness showed in her skin, no longer delicate and fine but nearly as dark as Mr. Roma's own; and in the stiff way she moved, as if her bones had bristled from lack of moisture. Even her eyes seemed parched, and caught in her dark eyebrows there was a fine spray of yellow dust from the road. Her beauty had changed, but it hadn't vanished.

Mr. Roma took off his gray fedora and held it over his heart.

"We'd better go back," Mrs. Wakefield said. "They will think I'm queer, coming out for a walk the woods like this as soon as I arrive. They don't know that John is buried here, do they?"

"I didn't tell them."

"It's just as well. They might be superstitious about death, especially the child." She smoothed the blossoms back over the stone until it was no longer visible. "Is she — is she very bright?"

"Oh, yes. But she has had no experience

— trains and zoos and airplanes and subways and movies, yes — she knows all about the artificial things — but here in the country she is always filled with wonder and fear. She has a tender heart. She loves everything that moves."

"What a pity." Mrs. Wakefield rose and brushed off the leaves that clung to her dress. The backs of her hands were baked and waffled by the sun. "She will grow up so suddenly and bitterly."

"No, no," Mr. Roma said, but he knew it was partly true. Jessie was too lavish with her love. She splattered it around like an inexperienced painter, and Mr. Roma often found daubs and splashes of it in the most unexpected places. "Jessie will grow up to be a fine woman, like you."

"Like me?" Her face twisted in a sudden grimace of pain. "God forbid."

Side by side they began to walk back toward the house, past Jessie's swing and the eucalyptus where the hummingbirds nested.

"I've changed, haven't I?" she said. "A lot."

"No more than any of us."

"A good deal more. I could see it in Carmelita's eyes — a really profound shock. She looked at me as if I were the one who had died, not Billy."

"Carmelita exaggerates things with her eyes," Mr. Roma said. "Luisa does too. It means nothing."

"I was a fool to come back. I should have kept moving." She shook her head as if to shake away the fact of her return. "They say tragedy ennobles people, gives them an inner peace. Well, I don't feel noble or peaceful. I feel angry, terribly and helplessly angry."

"It is all right to be angry."

"Not when you can't do anything about it except shake your fist at the sky and stamp your feet on the ground." She was silent a moment. "When I was Jessie's age my mother took me to a fortune-teller as a special treat. The old woman said, 'This child will have a long and happy life,' and for years and years I believed this with all my heart. Whenever I was depressed or lonely I would repeat those magic words to myself: *This child will have a long and happy life.* I often wish I could go back and find the old woman and thank her for the comfort she gave me. It was such a *personal* comfort — you understand? It wasn't like being told that God was in Heaven and would take care of me providing I was good. No, the old woman knew her business. Her words were clear and precise and confident, and there

53

were no strings attached, no provisos, like having to stop biting my fingernails and getting my pinafores dirty. This child was me, and the long and happy life was my irrevocable fate."

"You're still a young woman," Mr. Roma said anxiously, but she paid no attention to his remark.

She said, with an uncertain smile, "If I found the fortune-teller again, I don't know whether I'd call her a liar or ask her to repeat the words to me all over again."

"Maybe both."

"That's right, maybe both," she said. "But I've talked enough about my troubles. What will you do when the house is sold?"

Mr. Roma had been expecting the question. "We will go back to Marsalupe. We have saved money here. I am thinking we will open a small restaurant."

"A restaurant?"

"Only a very small one. A café."

"You've had no experience."

He glanced at her shyly. "I was thinking I would take one of these courses by mail — how to keep the books and what to buy. Carmelita will cook her special dishes like enchiladas, and beans with cheese, and tamales, and I will do the serving."

"It will be a very different life for you."

"Oh, yes. But better in some ways for Luisa. She doesn't like boarding at my sister's during the school months. And here, in the summer, it is too quiet for her." He nodded his head. "Yes, it is time for a change."

"Why?"

"You have looked after us too well, like children."

"It hasn't been a soft life."

"We have always been secure," he said gravely. "Good food and a nice place to live, not like the shacks in town where most of the colored people live."

"I would like to ask you to come with me, but I don't know where I'll be or what I'll be doing."

She looked out across the sea. The sun was going down, the sky was graying, and the water gleamed silver like the skin of a fish.

"I may go back to Mexico," she said. "There's a little place on the coast where Billy and I stayed, Manzanilla. We came back by boat. It was terribly hot. Even at night it didn't cool off, and I'd lie there with the portholes open, listening to the sea and wondering what was going to happen to Billy. Sometimes I couldn't manage him any more, he'd gotten so big, nearly a hundred pounds."

Mr. Roma nodded. He knew from experience how powerful Billy could be. Though he had tired easily, he'd had, at times, a tremendous strength.

"You remember how he liked to see things move?" Mrs. Wakefield said. "Well, he never got tired of watching the sea and the gulls. We found a little place near the stern where no one else ever went, and I'd sing to him or read aloud. He didn't understand all the words perhaps, but he understood that he was my son and I loved him."

When they came to the cypress hedge, the wind veered and brought with it the supper smells from the kitchen.

Mrs. Wakefield said, "You'd better call the little girl."

Hanging on a rusty nail in the shed was an old cowbell. Mr. Roma had found the cowbell years ago by the side of the road, but he had never been able to think of a use for it until Jessie came.

He brought the bell out and rang it loud enough to summon Jessie and to wake the dead.

5

"We'd have to ask her to have her meals with us," Evelyn said.

Mark finished buttoning his shirt and reached for the tweed jacket Evelyn had put out on the bed for him. "Why?"

"Well, we're sort of obliged to, aren't we? It'd be very ungracious not to."

Mark looked at her, rather irritably. "To be perfectly frank, I've never felt so ungracious in my whole life."

"But you like her all right, don't you?"

"I only exchanged two words with her. I don't know whether I like her or not."

"I actually thought you'd like company for a change. Instead of just Jessie and me."

"It depends on the company. Under the circumstances you can hardly expect her to scintillate."

"At least she's under control, no matter what she's feeling inside. Your collar's sticking up at the back."

"Thanks."

"I'll fix it."

Standing on tiptoe she smoothed the

57

collar down and ran her hand along the back of his neck.

"You need a haircut," she said. "We can drive into town some time on Monday."

He turned around and gave her a long careful look. "First this jacket business and now a haircut. For Mrs. Wakefield's benefit, I suppose?"

"Don't be silly. You've been getting haircuts all your life, why should you suddenly balk at getting another one?"

"I'm not balking. I'm merely thinking that some of the female vanities are amusing, if inconvenient."

"Vanity. Honestly, Mark!"

"That's what I call it," he said. "Enter Mrs. Wakefield and immediately you start dusting out corners and getting Jessie's ears washed and arranging a haircut for me."

"That's not vanity," she protested. "It's perfectly natural. All women do it."

"My point, exactly."

"Anyway, we're off the subject," Evelyn said, a little coldly. "Do we invite her to have her meals with us, or don't we?"

"Her plan was to eat with the Romas."

"But he's a — a —"

"Listen, these people have been living together for years. They've established their relationship, maybe a pretty subtle one.

We'd better keep out of it. If Mrs. Wakefield wants to eat with the Romas, let her."

"But it would seem terribly funny. I'd *feel* funny about it."

"Well, when you feel funny everybody else usually ends up feeling funny too, so do what you like."

She would have liked to challenge the statement, but she closed her lips firmly and pretended to be engrossed in straightening the scarf on the bureau and arranging Mark's brushes in perfect alignment. In the past week Mark had become less nervous and tense, but at the same time increasingly critical of her. She blamed it partly on herself and partly on the circumstance of their isolation. Mark had always been surrounded by people — his parents, and his sisters and the agents and writers and advertising men who streamed into his office wanting money or sympathy or reassurance or better contracts. Whatever they wanted Mark always tried to give them, but eventually he reached the point where his nerves began to crack and he had to get away for a while by himself. Once he was away from people, though, he began almost immediately to miss them. It seemed to Evelyn that she was expected to make up the loss and she couldn't do it. She didn't have the satiric intelligence Mark's sisters had, nor the neurotic wit of some of the writers and the agents Mark brought home for dinner. In comparison, she thought of herself as a rather colorless, phlegmatic creature, and she was always a little surprised when Mark found her amusing.

She glanced at him rather shyly, trying to estimate his mood and to see if he'd be interested in what she'd found out. "She's upstairs now, unpacking, in the room the nurse used to have."

"What nurse?"

"The one who lived with her. She was a real nurse too, not just a nursemaid."

"How do you know?"

"She left some things in the cupboard, a broken hypodermic syringe, for one."

"That isn't proof."

"There were other things too. The room itself is odd. I mean, it's so impersonal and bare, as if the person who lived in it had deliberately kept her personality out of it. It's a — well, a sort of *purposeful* room."

"You're a great little snooper," Mark said dryly. "So the nurse was a nurse. What of it?"

Evelyn looked faintly indignant. "I don't call it snooping. Naturally, when you rent a house you're curious about the people who

60

own it and who used to live there."

"So that's why you're inviting Mrs. Wakefield to eat with us. You're going to pump her, eh?"

"That's a nasty thing to say. I have no intention of asking her a single question."

Mark moved across the room, half-smiling. "I think I'll go for a walk. I'll take Jess along if she wants to go."

"I don't think she will. She's helping Mrs. Wakefield unpack.

"I warned Jessie —"

"I know, but Mrs. Wakefield *asked* her to help. She seems fond of children."

"All right, I'll go alone. Unless you want to come along?"

She knew it irked him to have to slow his walk down to her speed, so she said, "No, thanks. I'm going to set the table."

Every night before supper Mark used to climb down the cliff to the beach below the walk along the sand, or sit quietly by himself with the house and Jessie and Evelyn out of sight and out of mind.

There were two paths down the cliff. One was a hundred yards north of the house, where Mr. Roma had arranged a series of rough stone steps with a single guard rail of iron pipe. The other path was directly in front of the house and this was the one that

Jessie and Luisa and, sometimes, Mark, used. It was almost perpendicular, and the only way anyone could descend was by half-sitting, half-sliding down, clutching at the chaparral or jutting pieces of rock.

At the bottom of this path lay a heap of rubble and boulders left by landslides. A little to the south there was a giant over-hanging rock, where Mr. Roma kept the rowboat that he used for fishing. The high tides had worn away the bowels of the rock to make a cave whose walls were alive with scuttling crabs and mussels and baby aba-lones like little brown buttons glued to the walls of the cave.

It was on this rock that Mark liked to sit and listen to the gurgle of the water under-neath, and watch the cormorants that lived further along the cliff. There, the cliff was sheer rock, pitted with holes and ledges which housed the colony of sleek dark birds. Ceaselessly hungry, they clung to the ledges, their sharp eyes searching the sea for the splash of a fish.

By the time Mark reached the rock it was too dark to see the cormorants. The tide was out, and the sea seemed as quiet and thick as oil.

Whistling softly, he boosted himself up to the top of the rock. It was then that he saw

Luisa. She was sitting cross-legged in the sand and in one hand, very elegantly, she held a cigarette.

First Luisa blew all the smoke out of her mouth, and then out of her nose. Then, by way of experiment, she held one nostril closed and let the smoke pour out of the other. After a violent attack of coughing she crushed out the cigarette in the sand and put the butt in the pocket of her blouse.

"Hello," Mark said.

Luisa gave a wild little shriek.

"Sorry, I didn't mean to scare you."

"You scared me to *death*," Luisa cried. "You shouldn't scare people with bad hearts like I've got." Luisa could conjure up a fatal disease at the drop of a hat, and she frequently did, in the interests of drama. "I'll probably die young."

"That's too bad."

"I inherited it."

Mark said soberly, "Perhaps if you've got a bad heart you shouldn't smoke."

Luisa got up and brushed the sand off her skirt, watching Mark slyly out of the corner of her eye. "Are you going to tell on me?"

"No."

"Why not?"

Mark hesitated. "Well, I don't know why not. I suppose it's because I wouldn't like to get you in trouble. It might be a good idea if you didn't smoke until you're older, though."

"I don't smoke much. Only when I'm miserable and hate everyone. I ran away once. Two years ago."

"Where did you go?"

"Just to my aunt's house in San Diego. She married a white man. I was going to start my life all over, change my hair and my name. I was going to have a real English-sounding name like Jane Alice Fitzsimmons, something like that."

"Fitzsimmons is Irish, isn't it?"

Luisa shrugged. "It doesn't matter, Irish would be good enough. Anyway my aunt sent me back. Did you ever run away?"

"No," Mark said, smiling. "I wouldn't have stood a chance of getting far. I have five sisters."

"Five? Oh, I'd hate that. *I hate* women. Are they all married?"

"Three of them are. The other two work with me. We have sort of a family company."

"Mr. Wakefield didn't work at all," Luisa said. "He had money. Not her. She didn't have a cent. She was an ordinary school-teacher before she got married. When he died, though, she got the money."

"I didn't even know he was dead."

"He is, he died almost on this very spot."

She leaned her elbows on the rock and stared up at Mark. "It's funny you're Jessie's father."

"Why?"

"You're not like a *father*. You're more like, well, maybe a bandleader."

"Thanks," Mark said wryly. "Perhaps you don't know much about bandleaders."

Luisa's face indicated reproach. "It's my specialty in life. That's what I'm going to be some day, a singer with a band. First I wanted to be a nurse, like Miss Lewis. She was Billy's nurse. She was just wonderful, she knew everything. I'd like to know everything and go around saving people's lives, etcetera, and helping people. But I can't."

"You could try."

"It isn't just trying that counts. Nursing schools don't want people like me. Miss Lewis said that being colored doesn't matter, but she was wrong. It matters all the time, and everywhere, except right here."

"Why not here?"

"Mrs. Wakefield is different from other people."

In spite of the fact that the words sounded complimentary, Mark noticed the expression of repugnance on Luisa's face.

He said, "We'd better go back now, it's getting pretty dark."

"No, thanks," Luisa's voice was polite but firm. "I want to stay here."

"Come on. Your parents will be worried about you."

"No, they won't." She stood up straight again, rubbing one of her elbows where the skin was chafed from contact with the rock. "They'll be fussing around Mrs. Wakefield."

With a half-muffled snort of exasperation, Mark jumped down from the rock. "O.K. Stay here if you like."

He began walking briskly along the damp sand toward the stone steps, but he hadn't gone more than a hundred yards before he heard Luisa calling him:

"Mr. Banner! Wait, Mr. Banner!"

He turned around and waited, frowning, until she caught up with him.

"What changed your mind?"

"My matches are wet. They wouldn't light."

"That's just too bad."

"I was going to stay down here practically all night so I wouldn't have to be nice to Mrs. Wakefield."

"Why don't you want to be nice to her?"

"Because *they* are," Luisa said scornfully. "My parents, I mean. They're always making such a fuss over her. I'll be glad when she leaves."

He paused at the bottom of the steps for

Luisa to go up ahead of him. He saw that she was shivering, and the skin of her bare arms was tinged with mauve in the twilight.

"Mr. Banner, do you believe that a person can be terribly nice on the surface and still have bad things inside them that come out in their children?"

"No," Mark said. "Come on now, make it fast. You're getting cold."

When they reached the top of the steps they saw that most of the lights in the house were on, and the Japanese lanterns in the patio had been lit.

"I was supposed to help with supper," Luisa said bitterly. "Now everybody'll be mad at me, everybody."

"Well, I'm not."

"You sounded mad, down there," Luisa said. "Kind of like James Mason."

Mark didn't know who James Mason was, but he felt vaguely uncomfortable under Luisa's stare. He was glad when they reached the house and she ducked away, around the side of it, bent double to avoid the patio lights.

Evelyn was sitting on the stone half-wall, smoking cigarette. Her slight delicate figure, and the fluff of bangs over her forehead made her look more childish and virginal than Luisa. At his approach she stood up and threw away the cigarette. She had put on a fresh dress, a blue-and-white printed silk that brought out the blue in her eyes and showed off her new tan.

"Have a nice walk?"

"No."

"I thought I saw Luisa with you," Evelyn said. "Everyone's been looking for her."

"I bumped into her down by the rock."

"That must have been fun."

She smiled, but she had a sudden sick feeling at the pit of her stomach. In all their twelve years of marriage, she had never been able to get over these quick spasms of jealousy. She had always prided herself on being a reasonable woman. Her jealousy worried her because it was so capricious and unjust, and it had no relation to the facts. It was impossible to be jealous of Mark talking to a fifteen-year-old girl; but the feeling was there, a lost helpless sensation.

Holding on tight to her smile, she said, "What did you talk about? There are some martinis in the pitcher on the table."

"I'll have one," Mark said. "She talked, I stooged. She can be rather interesting when she forgets to put on those adolescent histrionics."

"Such as?" Evelyn said brightly. "What'd she say?"

"This and that. You don't seriously want to know, do you?"

"Well, we haven't got anything else much to talk about right now, have we? We might as well talk about Luisa. Or a good book. Have you read any good books lately?"

Mark shook his head. "No. Have a martini?"

"Thanks."

He brought the drink over to her. "Now let's have it. What's on your mind?"

"Nothing. Absolutely nothing!"

"Cross your heart?"

"And hope to die."

"That's fine." Balancing his own glass and hers, he leaned down and kissed the tip of her ear. "Sometimes you get some peculiar ideas."

She flashed him a bright, empty smile.

"Don't I just," she said cheerfully.

Mrs. Wakefield came out from the living room. She was still wearing the yellow knit dress but she had put on a topaz necklace, and her hair was combed straight back from her forehead and caught in a barrette at the nape of her neck.

There was a certain new buoyancy in her walk as she crossed the patio holding Jessie by the hand. Under the soft lights of the lanterns her hair glowed, rich and velvety, and her face was quite animated, as if the contact with old friends and the excitement of meeting new people had stimulated her, and restored her youth.

"It looks like a party," she said. "You shouldn't have gone to so much trouble, Mrs. Banner."

Though she addressed Evelyn, it was Mark she looked at. He had paid little attention to her when they first met in the afternoon, and he was surprised now to see how tall she was — nearly as tall as he — and how full of energy her body looked. No — more than energy. Challenge. She herself seemed ignorant of the challenge; she was friendly, impersonal. But he felt a little thrill of interest run through his veins, and he looked away deliberately when their eyes met, aware that Evelyn was watching him and could see the invisible.

"It *is* a party," said Jessie, who could make a party out of a piece of cake or a picnic out of a hard-boiled egg eaten on the beach. "Daddy, do I look different?"

"Let me see," Mark said. "Well, yes. You're terribly clean for one thing."

"No, this is *much* differenter."

"Your hair's combed."

"No! This is *much* better!"

"Then I guess it's the earrings."

Jessie bobbed her head up and down, and the gold earrings swung deliciously against her skin.

"I hope you don't mind?" Mrs. Wakefield said to Evelyn. "She saw them in my case, and I thought just this once — ?"

Evelyn minded quite a bit; to her Jessie looked grotesque in the gypsy earrings. But she said pleasantly, "Of course not. As long as Jessie doesn't try to make a habit of it."

"I won't make a habit. I promise."

"But don't keep shaking your head like that, Jessie. You look like an idiot."

"What's an idiot?"

"Someone who isn't very bright."

"What causes idiots?"

"I don't know. Lots of things, I guess."

Mrs. Wakefield spoke suddenly in a high, unnatural voice: "I'd better go and say hello to Luisa. She might think I've forgotten her."

"I'm an idiot," Jessie cried, rolling her head dramatically from side to side. "Look, I'm an idiot!"

But Mrs. Wakefield wouldn't look. Averting her eyes, she walked back into the house with quick nervous strides.

It was nearly half an hour before she returned, full of apologies, and apparently at ease again.

"You didn't keep us waiting," Evelyn said. "As a matter of fact, Mark likes to eat late anyway."

Her expression didn't change, though she couldn't help wondering why it had required so much time to "say hello" to Luisa, and why Mrs. Wakefield had decided to remove the topaz necklace she'd been wearing when she came downstairs.

6

When dinner was over Mark built a fire in the living room grate. He had done considerable talking during the meal, mostly about his work, and he was feeling well pleased with himself, and with Mrs. Wakefield. Her interest seemed genuine, and her comments had been unexpectedly intelligent. He tried to tell himself that these were the reasons why he found her pleasing, though he was increasingly conscious of a feeling of excited curiosity.

But Jessie was bored. The effect of the earrings, which had temporarily imposed on her an adult restraint, was wearing off. When Mrs. Wakefield settled down in a wing chair in front of the fireplace, Jessie crowded in beside her, in spite of a perfectly obvious frown from her father. Her parents had all sorts of ways of communicating their displeasure without words — coughs and raised eyebrows and gestures and frowns and sometimes even little pinches if the situation was desperate — but Jessie had a way of either ignoring these hints with a blank stare, or else bringing them right out into the open arena with a blunt question: *What are you frowning at me for? What am I doing?* Jessie had a sophisticated subtlety which was all the more effective because it hid behind her age, and no one could prove it was there.

"Can you play any games?" Jessie said. "Like parchesi or old maid or hearts?"

Mrs. Wakefield smiled. "I used to, but I'm afraid I've forgotten how."

"Don't you play games with your little boy?"

"Not any more."

"If you could bring him along next time, I could teach him how to play casino."

"That's nice of you, Jessie. But I'm afraid I can't bring him."

"Why?"

"Isn't it just about your bedtime, Jess?" Mark interrupted. "Scoot on up now and don't forget to clean your teeth."

Jessie looked pained. "Well, what are you making such *faces* at me for? I didn't do anything!"

"You heard me. Now for once in your life go to bed without arguing."

"I want to know why she can't bring her little boy."

"Well, you see, Jessie," Mrs. Wakefield

said patiently, "Billy had a bad accident."

"In a car?"

"No, a boat. He was drowned."

Jessie asked, frowning, "Couldn't he swim?"

"No."

"I can swim. In a pool, not in the ocean, on account of the waves."

"We'll have to go swimming in the ocean together. The waves won't hurt you if you know how to handle them."

"Can we go tomorrow?"

"If you'll go to bed right now."

"I will."

Mrs. Wakefield unscrewed the gold earrings. Jessie was secretly relieved to be rid of them. Her head felt so delightfully light and airy that, even after she was all undressed and tucked in, it wouldn't stay down on the pillow properly. It kept wanting to bob up again like the balloons she used to play with in Central Park when she tried to hold them under water.

She closed her eyes, wondering why Billy hadn't bobbed up again like that. But she couldn't go to sleep. There were the sounds of voices from the living room beneath her, tantalizing sounds, almost but not quite loud enough for her to identify words. Outside her window a mockingbird rustled through the oleanders and challenged her with her own name, calling "OO-essie!" Just the way Carmelita called her up from the beach sometimes.

She got up in the dark and went to the window. From the yard below, very faintly, came the sound of James scraping his bill insistently against the screen door. The lights were on in Luisa's room over the garage, and she could see Luisa quite clearly standing in front of the bureau mirror. Luisa had her hair done up on top of her head and she was wearing nothing but a slip and a necklace.

Jessie leaned away out of the window and called in a soft penetrating whisper, "Luisa! Hey, Luisa!"

"OO-essie, oo-essie," the mockingbird corrected sharply. "OO-essie, oo-essie!"

"Luisa!"

She had to call several times before Luisa finally heard her. She turned off the light and came to the window, propping her elbows on the sill. "What do you want?"

"Nothing. What are you doing?"

"None of your business," Luisa said crossly. "You're supposed to go to sleep, it's nine o'clock."

"We could talk."

"I don't want to talk, I'm busy."

"What doing?"

"None of your business."

"You sound funny," Jessie said with a little shiver of excitement. Luisa's voice was ghostly, it seemed to rise mysteriously from the velvet darkness like fog from the sea. "Do I sound funny too?"

"Sorta."

"I found the you-know-what in the woods today. The — dead man."

"You weren't supposed to," Luisa said. "It's a secret."

"Why?"

"Because he's in hell fire."

"I don't believe it," Jessie said, shaken. "My mother says there's no such place as hell fire."

"She doesn't know. She's not a Catholic."

"Why did he go to hell fire?"

"You're too little to know. He did, that's all. There are rules about it and he broke one."

"Do you ever break any?"

"Lots," Luisa said recklessly. "I'll probably go to hell too, only I don't care. It can't be much worse than being stuck out here with not even a human being to talk to."

"You can talk to me."

"Oh, you. I meant, real *people*. Boys and men mostly. I hate women."

"Maybe you could get married."

77

"I intend to, don't worry. I already got a boy friend."

"I might get married myself," Jessie said thoughtfully. "Maybe if Billy hadn't of drowned I could marry him."

"Billy?" Luisa let out a noise that sounded like a muffled giggle, and a moment later she slammed the window shut and pulled down the blind.

Moving softly across the room in her bare feet, Jessie turned on the lamp on the bureau. It was here she kept her most important treasures, a clown sachet that smelled of lilacs, odds and ends of shells and colored pebbles, and a family of tiny rubber dolls living in an abalone shell, each of them no bigger than Jessie's little finger. Holding the place of honor in the center of the bureau was the baby starfish housed in one of Carmelita's glass casseroles.

It was a most unusual starfish, everyone agreed, because most starfish had just five or six arms, but Jessie's had eleven and a half. Jessie called it Cinderella and anticipated the day when it would recognize her and come over to the side of the bowl in response to its name. So far the starfish had done nothing but sit in the sand at the bottom of the bowl, ignoring its lavish banquet of bread crumbs and rice krispies and sowbugs and sea lettuce. But Jessie knew this was because it felt strange in front of a strange little girl, just as she had felt on the first day of school. She was fiercely convinced that it would soon get over its shyness and respond to her overwhelming love and tenderness.

"Cinderella," Jessie whispered, tapping the side of the bowl very gently. "Here, Cinderella. Come on."

She was almost certain that Cinderella moved an arm languidly in reply, but she couldn't be sure; the water was so murky with disintegrated food that Cinderella looked like a delicate pink brooch accidentally dropped into the bowl.

It was possible that since it was after nine o'clock Cinderella might be sleeping. Jessie didn't want to disturb it, but she did want it to move just a little to dispel the vague fear that was pressing against her heart.

"Cinderella, it's me, it's Jessie Banner."

She tapped the glass again with her fingernails, and this time she was sure that there was no movement at all except a tiny ripple of water that danced to the other side of the bowl and back again.

She pulled out the second bottom drawer of the bureau, and using the edge of it as a stool to stand on, she peered anxiously down into the dingy water. The sea smell of the water mingled sickeningly with the lilac sachet and the sharp acrid odor of the abalone shell.

"Cinderella," Jessie said. "Look where I am now, up here."

Putting her hand into the water she touched one of Cinderella's fragile beaded arms, and then slowly she drew the starfish out. It lay, soft and cold, in the palm of her hand. The tiny hairs along its arms didn't wave and tickle her skin the way they had when she'd first picked it out of the tide pool.

After a moment she put it back into the water. It sank to the bottom and she realized, not only that it was dead, but that all her plans and hopes for it had been futile. It had never been just shy and sleepy; it had never heard her calling, or seen her, or known she was Jessie Banner; it had never eaten the bread crumbs and the sowbugs, or been aware of its snug little home in the casserole; it had never liked her.

With a cry she picked up the casserole and climbed down from the drawer. Some of the water spilled on her nightgown and the wet cloth stuck to her skin, quite cold at first but getting warmer and warmer until she hardly noticed the wetness. Without turning on the hall light she crept down the stairs holding the heavy bowl awkwardly in her arms. The smell of the water nauseated her, it had become the smell of death; and the starfish at the bottom was no longer Cinderella, cunningly and delicately made like a breathing flower. It was a dead thing that Jessie couldn't bear to see or to touch. The real Cinderella lay close against Jessie's heart, and she could keep it safe there only by getting rid of this impostor.

The voices from the living room were quite distinct now but she didn't stop to eavesdrop. Slowly and silently she went through the dark hall and the dining room with her burden, not sure yet what she intended to do with it.

She pressed open the swinging door into the kitchen, squinting her eyes against the sudden dazzle of light.

Carmelita was finishing the dishes, humming to herself. In the platform rocker by the window Mr. Roma sat reading the newspaper. His glasses were perched in the middle of his nose as if they had alighted there by accident and meant to fly away at any minute.

He held the paper at arm's length, frowning at it over the top of his glasses. These newspaper people were getting very careless lately about the printing. In spite of the spectacles Carmelita had given him for Christmas he found it difficult to make out the furry letters.

"Bless my buttons," he said in surprise. "It's Jessie."

Jessie put the bowl on the floor and wiped her hands very carefully on her nightgown.

"This is a little visit, eh?" Mr. Roma said, taking off his glasses. "The starfish is hungry again?"

Jessie stared at him, mute and suffering.

"I told you, Jessie. I said to you, this little fellow cannot live in a bowl; no, he must have the whole sea, he cannot breathe unless the waves stir up the water."

"I made waves. I stirred it up."

"The whole sea," Mr. Roma said again. "I am sorry."

"It was only a fish anyway, just a plain old fish."

But her voice trembled, and Mr. Roma understood that of the billions of fish in the sea this one alone had been raised from anonymity by Jessie's love. In all the seven seas there was not another one quite like it and never would be.

"Carmelita," Mr. Roma said, "is there a small piece of cake left from supper?"

"I don't want any cake, thank you," Jessie said.

"A very small piece?"

"No." She couldn't explain to him that eating a piece of cake would only make her feel worse because ordinarily she would have shared it with Cinderella, floating the crumbs very cautiously so as not to frighten it.

"Not hungry, eh?"

"No."

"Come, stand on the rug. Your feet will get cold."

"I could sit on your knee."

"Yes, I guess you could."

She sat on his knee but it turned out to be quite bony and uncomfortable, and after a moment she got off again and stood hesitantly on the braided cotton rug.

"I could bury it," she said finally. "Like the man in the woods, with a stone to show where."

"It's too late to do it now."

"No, it isn't. I'm not tired, I'm not hungry or cold or sleepy or anything. People always think I am when I'm not. Anyway it won't take long. It would just take a *little* hole, Cinderella is so *little*."

She blinked away the sudden tears that stung her eyelids. Mr. Roma saw them anyway.

"It won't take us a minute," he said.

Carmelita muttered in Spanish that it was not good, such play-acting about death; it would bring more bad luck to a house already loaded down with it.

Mr. Roma rebuked her softly: "Houses don't have luck. Only people have. And then, who can say, until the very end, what has been good luck and what has been bad luck?"

"The priest can. You talk like an infidel."

"Ah, now." He took the flashlight out of the cupboard and handed it to Jessie. Then he picked up the bowl from the floor, wrinkling his nose a little at the smell.

Jessie opened the screen door for him, holding the flashlight, and looking very solemn and pale, like an acolyte in her white nightgown. She looked so different that James didn't recognize her. He turned and waddled away, squawking, into the shadows.

"Play-acting," Carmelita repeated with scorn, but she followed them out on the porch, wiping her hands on her apron. To bury this soulless animal in the ground like a man was a sin, and never again would she use the glass casserole, never. She would hide it in the shed and pretend she had mislaid it. Or she would throw it over the steep cliff where the cormorants lived and the next high tide would carry away the pieces

84

or grind them to dust on the rocks below the cliff.

Standing on the dark porch she crossed herself, her flabby face lifted toward the cold bright eyes of heaven.

"Here," Jessie said. "Under my window."

"That would be suitable."

Mr. Roma dug the hole himself, using a little stick to pry loose the hard dry ground beside the oleander.

"Tomorrow," he said, chipping at the earth, "tomorrow, maybe Mrs. Wakefield will find you a new starfish, a bigger prettier one."

"No, thank you."

"Mrs. Wakefield knows all about the things in the sea. She will fix the starfish for you so you can take it home with you and show to your friends. Of course it will not be alive," he added apologetically, "but it will look so."

"It won't move, though."

"No. But it will be pretty to put on your dresser and use as a pin cushion."

"I don't have any pins."

"Even so," he said briskly, "it will be pretty to look at and remind you of the sea."

"How big will it be?"

"Big as your head."

"Bless my buttons," Jessie said. "I'd like one like that."

"Tomorrow. The very first thing to-morrow. You're a very sensible girl. Already you know something some people never learn — when you lose one thing you must accept a substitute and be cheerful about it."

Jessie didn't quite understand what he meant but she was warmed by his approval. She felt impervious to the cold slap of the wind.

Leaning back on his heels, Mr. Roma said, "There now, it is all ready. You bring the little starfish."

Jessie tipped the water out of the bowl. It oozed out slowly, thick with the soggy bread crumbs and the slimy sea lettuce and the sowbugs that floated like little black boats down a sluggish river. She picked up the starfish, pretending it was only a flower she'd found unexpectedly on the ground.

She put it into the hole Mr. Roma had dug, and he covered it up very quickly and neatly. To mark the grave he pressed into the ground with his heel a white pebble with gray stripes; and beside the pebble he laid an oleander blossom, no longer fresh but still showing signs of pink under its sun-seared edges.

"You feel better now," Mr. Roma stated. "I know how it is. The starfish is buried and

86

already it has become part of the past. Maybe you're already planning how you will tell your friends about it, eh? 'Once I had a little starfish,' you will say. 'He was a pretty little fellow but he died, and it was nobody's fault.' "

"I'll tell them he drowned."

"Oh, no. Now that isn't right. No, a starfish cannot drown. He died for lack of air."

"It looked like he was drowned, like Billy."

Mr. Roma glanced at her quickly. "Who said that Billy was drowned?"

"Mrs. Wakefield."

"No, no, I'm quite sure you're mistaken, Jessie. Maybe you didn't understand her. Maybe she said, Billy is *dead*."

"She told me herself that he had a bad accident, he was drowned."

"Well." He stood for a moment, scuffing the ground with the toe of his shoe like a hesitant child. Then he turned and picked up the empty bowl. "Come along now. It's getting late."

She took his free hand and walked along beside him with her nightgown flapping around her legs and pushing her along like a sail in the wind.

Carmelita was waiting for them at the kitchen door. She had taken the scarf off her head for the night and her hair bristled with bobby pins like a porcupine. Her voice bristled too, with sharp staccato Spanish:

"Leave the casserole on the steps. I will not have it in the house."

"Is she mad?" Jessie said anxiously to Mr. Roma.

"No, no. She wants me to leave the bowl outside."

"Why?"

"It smells a little." He put the bowl on the steps and opened the screen door.

The kitchen was warm and alive with lights. The lights splashed like acid into Jessie's eyes and they watered feebly and wouldn't stay open.

"The little one's tired," Carmelita said reprovingly. "All this play-acting, all this night air. What will her mother and father have to say about this?"

"We will be very quiet," Mr. Roma said. "Eh, Jessie? Can we go upstairs very, very quiet?"

"I can go up by myself. You have squeaky shoes on."

"You're a sensible girl."

"Good night, Mr. Roma."

"Good night, Jessie."

She slipped out through the swinging door, through the dining room and into the hall. As she ducked past the doorway of the living room she had a glimpse of Mrs. Wakefield sitting at the piano. Her right arm hung straight down at her side, as if it was broken, and with her left hand she was playing soft, low chords, humming the melody absentmindedly, her eyes half-closed. Her voice brushed softly against the air, like spider webs.

When she reached her room again Jessie closed the door tight. The wet patch on her nightgown had dried, and there was nothing to show that she'd been downstairs at all except the empty spot on the bureau where the casserole had been.

She tried to keep from looking at it as she switched off the lamp, but the gap was there even in the dark. She couldn't escape from it any more than she could escape from the gap in her mouth when she lost a tooth. A new tooth always grew in its place, but the period of loss, of ugliness, was never quite forgotten.

Tomorrow, she thought. *Tomorrow.*

It was like a present under the tree at Christmas. It couldn't be actually opened ahead of time, but it could be wondered about, shaken, smelled, touched on the outside, the ribbons loosened a little, the paper pierced with peepholes.

She went to bed hugging the box of to-morrow with its new starfish, not yet found, and the piece of chocolate cake waiting in the cake box, and the swim in the sea with Mrs. Wakefield. She had a transient feeling of contempt for the boy Billy who couldn't even swim.

7

Mrs. Wakefield turned from the piano, rubbing her hands as if to restore their warmth and flexibility. "I'm badly out of practice. I haven't touched a piano for over a year."

"I don't play at all," Mark said. "It sounds wonderful to me."

Mrs. Wakefield got up, making a funny little grimace of protest. "I could never play very well, just enough to be able to read notes if I looked at them long and hard enough. I didn't start to learn, actually, until after my son was born and we came here to live. My son was very fond of music."

"Jessie isn't. She can't sing two notes."

"Oh, Billy didn't sing. He liked to listen though, he would listen for hours while I played — I hope I'm not keeping you up? Am I?"

"Of course not." Mark was faintly annoyed at Evelyn, curled up on the davenport and looking so uncompromisingly sleepy.

"I shouldn't have said Billy didn't sing," Mrs. Wakefield corrected. "Actually he did, only they were his own songs. Some of them

91

were very unusual." She added with a laugh, "I'm talking my head off tonight, I haven't talked so much for a long time."

It was true that she had talked a lot but it seemed to Mark that she had deliberately said nothing. The trivialities, the vague references to Billy and her husband slipped off the surface of her mind leaving the rest undisturbed. Mark did not share Evelyn's unreserved curiosity — with perfect guilelessness Evelyn bartered secrets with the elevator boy, the butcher, the news vendor — but he was intrigued by Mrs. Wakefield's intentional deviousness. He felt that it was not natural to her, that she was, in fact, a rather candid woman who was afraid of indulging her candor.

She was his own age, but he felt awkward and inexperienced in her presence. Even when she gazed directly at him, her eyes were disinterested, as if they had seen a little of everything in this world and had already looked across a dreary space into the next.

"It's been a year now since I've really talked to anyone," she said. "Billy and I were traveling, you know. We went here and there, all over, but we never met anyone we knew, so all the talking we did was to each other."

Traveling, Mark thought, where and how?

Train, plane, rocket ship? Argentina, Trinidad, Manila, Siberia, Little America? And why take an eight- or nine-year-old boy out of school for a year to go traveling? Mark thought of the noisy nerve-racking trip across the country with Jessie tearing through the train like a tornado, picking up and laying down an endless débris of people, discarded magazines and newspapers, Pepsi-Cola treasure tops, and small nomadic and anonymous children over whom she assumed a position of benevolent tyranny.

"It must have been hard traveling with a child," he said.

"Sometimes. But Billy was usually very patient. And we had things to do, like lessons. I used to teach school."

"Luisa told me."

"Luisa loves to give out information," she said wryly. "Sometimes, I warn you, it isn't accurate. She has all kinds of fancies, superstitions, like her mother. Carmelita is one of these half-Catholics, you know. She was brought up very strictly but she no longer goes to church except on Easter. It is terrible around here at Easter time with Carmelita teetering on the brink of hell. I'm often tempted to push her over, but no, I can't. She is a good woman —" She broke off suddenly as if she realized she had stepped over the invisible line she'd drawn for herself. When her foot touched the line a bell rang a warning. "I mustn't keep you up any longer."

"I'm not a bit tired," Evelyn said, suddenly opening her eyes very wide as proof. "Let me make some more martinis."

"No, thanks. No, really. You've been awfully kind to bother about me at all. I'd almost forgotten I'm supposed to be here on business. I've never taken an inventory before, but I bought a notebook at the dime store, and a pencil. I guess that's all the equipment I need." She turned to Mark with a frank smile. "The object of it, I suppose, is to make sure you don't walk out with something when you leave."

"I assure you we won't."

"It's all very silly. I have nothing of value, here or anywhere."

She shook hands with them both. Her touch was firm, the skin of her hand cold and dry.

When she had left the room Mark experienced a vague let-down. He looked at Evelyn, straightening the cushions on the davenport and gathering up the ash trays, and she seemed quite commonplace, an ordinary pretty little housewife performing her ordinary duties after the departure of a guest.

"Don't fuss around," he said. "Carmelita can do that in the morning."

"I'm not fussing. I always do this."

"That's the point. Let's vary it a little."

"All right." She put down the ash tray she had just picked up, jarring some of the ashes out on the coffee table. "I seem to have annoyed you in some way. God knows I'm getting to be quite an expert at it."

"You didn't have to droop around all evening like a dying violet."

"Mrs. Wakefield doesn't have the same adrenalin effect on me that she has on you."

"What does that mean, exactly?"

"Nothing," Evelyn said. "It's just a reply to the dying violet theme."

"If you're hinting that I paid too much attention to her, kindly remember that you were the one who wanted to have her around. I like her," he said, as if surprised at himself. "I think she's had some tough breaks."

"But you wouldn't feel *quite* so sorry for her if she had three eyes."

"So you're jealous again, are you?"

"Observant, not jealous. Obviously she's an attractive woman, even if she is old enough to be your mother."

The statement was so ridiculous that

Mark smiled in spite of himself. "Aren't you exaggerating a little?"

"Maybe."

"Come here a minute."

"No." She shook her head obstinately. "I don't want any of your conciliatory pecks on the forehead. The hell with it."

"I hadn't the slightest intention —"

"Yes, you had. We're always having these pat little kiss-and-make-up scenes. I'm tired of them, they don't settle anything."

"What does?"

"I don't know. A heart-to-heart talk maybe."

"If all the heart-to-heart talks we've had were laid end to end —"

"Oh, I know." She frowned and then smoothed away the frown with the tips of her fingers. "Well," she said finally, "you don't mind if I stagger upstairs now like a dying violet?"

"For God's sake, stop repeating that."

"Why? I like it. It suits me. I *feel* like one, sort of shriveled and limp and curled in at the toes."

"I'm sorry I had to pick the one phrase in the English language that got your goat."

"You can have my goat," Evelyn said. "Keep it. There's plenty more where that came from."

Mark looked at her in surprise. "Why all this sudden cynicism?"

"You started it. You said, stop fussing around."

"There's nothing so awful about that."

"I know, but it's a sign."

"Certainly it's a sign. It's a sign that I didn't want you fussing around."

"No," she said. "It's more than that. You're bored with me. Maybe you always have been, but it didn't show so much until we came here. I've gotten the feeling lately that you expect me to be a lot of things I'm not — you know, very clever and sharp and terribly, terribly amusing."

"I didn't marry you for laughs."

She said quietly, "We can't discuss the problem if you won't even admit there is one."

"I'll be damned if I'll admit something that isn't so." His denial sounded convincing though he knew that she was at least partly right. "You seem to think the problem is that I've lost interest in you and you consequently get jealous when I show an interest in any other woman. Is that it?"

"That's close enough."

"Since you have it all figured out, tell me why I've suddenly lost interest in you."

"I'm beginning to think you never had

any. Maybe that's why I've always been jealous of you. No, don't interrupt. I don't blame you. I suppose the real trouble is that I'm not very interesting. Nothing much has ever happened to me. I can't go around being dark and mysterious and fascinating like *her*." She raised her voice, in a crude imitation of Mrs. Wakefield's. "My dear, I haven't touched a piano since the time I played 'Pop Goes the Weasel' for those headhunters in Borneo, yackity, yackity, yackity." She turned away, abruptly. "Sorry. I guess I've been hitting the catnip too hard lately."

"Evelyn . . ."

"I'm going to bed."

"Wait just a minute. You're not actually jealous of her any more, now that we've talked the matter over. Are you?"

"Oh, Lord. You and your simple faith in words. It's touching. Why shouldn't I be jealous of her?"

"Because I've told you you have no reason to be."

"All right then. I'm not jealous. Does that ease your mind any?"

"Not a damn bit, thanks."

"You know, I'm such a simple-minded creature that things look simple to me. Like this, for instance. I love you and you don't love me, and Jessie is caught in the middle, somewhere in the middle where she hasn't anything to hang on to. We're not a *family* — you know what I mean? — and sometimes I think, I can't help thinking, that Jessie knows that, and that she hates us both." She rubbed her eyes. They were a little pink, a little too bright. "Good night, Mark. You might think it over."

"I'll try. Good night."

While he was getting ready for bed he thought about Evelyn and Jessie for a little while but he couldn't keep his mind on them. Mrs. Wakefield's image kept looming up, and he found himself remembering, and puzzling over, some of her odd, half-restrained gestures — like those of an actress, he thought, whose freedom of movement and expression was being constantly controlled by an unseen director.

Yet he realized that it was unfair to judge her by normal standards. She had recently lost a child, and to make it worse, the child had been her only son. *My son was very fond of music.... Billy and I were traveling here and there.... Billy was usually very patient.... He was drowned.*

In fact, Mark thought, she talked quite freely about Billy, but the more she said the more elusive he became, like an old photograph, faded and faceless.

He switched off the light and groped his way to the bed.

It was nearly morning when he was awakened by the sharp yelping of a sea lion. The sound was like one of Jessie's wild cries of excitement, but there was a note of hysteria in it, a wild regret.

After a minute the sea lion stopped abruptly and Mark went back to sleep. But the noise crept into his dreams, changing identity — it was Jessie shouting, a dog howling, a woman sobbing; it was a faceless little boy barking from a rock in the sea, half-hidden in the slimy eel grass.

Later in the morning, after breakfast, Mark remembered the sea lion and asked Mr. Roma if he had heard it.

"Sea lion?" Mr. Roma said. "Oh, no, we don't have sea lions along here. Over at the island, yes, there are hundreds of them."

"I heard one."

Mr. Roma shrugged. "If you heard one, then that is very unusual."

He went off down the path, lurching slightly under the weight of the pails of chicken mash.

8

Slowly the pages were being covered with Mrs. Wakefield's untidy printing.

Contents of Dining Room: one bleached-mahogany dining set, table, buffet, eight chairs, value about $800? Two pairs damask drapes and rods — value perhaps $200, but this may be too high. One 12x18 Sultana-land rug, value, I've had it for years and it's worn in spots. Couldn't be worth more than $400, not that perhaps. . . .

She couldn't write down even the contents of a room without stamping each article with her personality.

"For the rug, five hundred," Mr. Roma said. "And you must not write little notes like that. It isn't businesslike."

"How else can I show that I don't know the actual value?"

"Put little question marks. For example, if you are quite uncertain put one question mark, and if you are very uncertain put two or three question marks."

"That doesn't sound so businesslike either."

"Still, it is *more* so, eh?"

"I guess."

"Now. Six pictures."

"They're only reproductions, forty dollars at the most."

"Fifty," he said briskly. "Consider the frames. Myself, I would demand a hundred, considering the frames."

Mrs. Wakefield pushed her hair back off her forehead and printed: $50 ???

"Two silver candelabra," Mr. Roma said. "You had a bad dream last night?"

"Yes."

"Like in the old days."

"Did I — make a noise?"

"Mr. Banner heard you. He thought it was a sea lion."

"A sea lion." She looked up at him with a queer little laugh. "That's rather funny. I hope I didn't disturb anyone else."

"I didn't hear you myself, but I remembered your old nightmares."

"I woke up crying. It's a strange thing to wake up, thinking you've been sleeping soundly, and find tears still wet on your cheeks and your throat aching. . . . They aren't nightmares," she added quietly. "They are things that really happened. I live them over again."

"They are not out of focus?"

102

"Sometimes the faces are distorted, and the house, when I see it in a dream, looks different, very high and narrow like a witch's castle; but the things that happen are real. They are worse than nightmares, more lasting and terrifying."

She picked up the pencil again and printed: two silver candelabra. "They were a wedding present, I haven't any idea how much they're worth, or even whether they're solid silver."

He tested their weight, frowning in concentration. "They must be solid silver. Three hundred dollars at least, eh?"

"Perhaps."

"One silver coffee set and tray. You didn't tell me that Billy was drowned."

"Didn't I? I thought I had."

"No. No, you didn't."

"It's no secret. It was in some of the papers."

"How did he drown?"

"It was when we were coming back from Manzanilla. He fell off the — over the railing. There's no use talking about it. It's finished."

"But you . . ."

"I won't talk about it."

"You talk about things to yourself when you're dreaming," Mr. Roma said. "That is worse."

She said bitterly, "At least if I talk to myself it won't go any further."

"But it does. You cry in the night, and people will ask, why? What has this woman got on her mind? What are her sad secrets?"

"Oh, stop it!" She flung the pencil across the table. He stooped immediately and picked it up; the gesture seemed deliberately and cynically servile.

"No secrets," she said. "There's simply nothing more to tell you. He was playing on deck. It was very hot, and I left him for a minute to get him a glass of water from the cooler. When I came back he had fallen overboard. No one saw it happen, no one heard him cry out, nothing. It was as if he never existed."

"I am sorry," Mr. Roma said. He felt questions stirring in the back of his mind, but they weren't ready yet to be put into words.

"I looked for him all over the ship before I could bring myself to believe he'd fallen overboard. By the time the ship had turned and made a search it was too late."

"You should have told me this yesterday."

"Why? What difference does it make now?"

"It makes me think you were planning not to tell me at all."

"What nonsense!" She smiled with sudden candor. "You're becoming very fanciful, Carl."

She had never called him anything but Mr. Roma, and the use of his first name seemed like a warning to him: *Step back, Carl, where you belong. We are old friends but the terms of the friendship have always been set by me.*

It was as if she was reminding him that times had changed; she didn't live there any more and they no longer had that mutual dependence that exists, apart from class or race, among people living together in a lonely place.

He gave her back the pencil. "One set of Spode china," he said.

"It doesn't work out, this verbal sharing of burdens. Do you feel any better now that you know about Billy? Do *I* feel any better for having told you? It doesn't work out," she repeated. "There are some pieces missing from the Spode, aren't there?"

"Two cups and the cream pitcher."

"I — let's leave this for awhile. I can't do any more right now."

She got up and went to the window, her arms folded across her breasts. "You're like a child in some ways, Mr. Roma. Things look either black or white to you. It's all very simple, not having to classify the other shades in the color chart. Like a child," she said again. "If you like people you must approve of everything they do, they must be perfect. I feel that you're censuring me because I went to get Billy a glass of water."

"No, I am puzzled."

There was a long silence before she turned from the window and spoke again. "The tide's going out. It will be a good time to find Jessie a starfish."

"She is all ready and waiting on the beach. Luisa is with her." With an air of deliberation, he said, "The necklace you gave Luisa is very pretty. Very expensive."

"I meant to bring her something and I forgot," Mrs. Wakefield said coolly. "So I gave her the necklace."

"What is Luisa to do in return?"

"Not a thing."

"I must ask her to give it back to you."

"Why?"

He looked carefully down at the floor as if he expected to find an answer written there less blurred and elusive than the one in his mind. "Well, it is too expensive a gift for a young girl, for one thing."

"But it's my money. If I choose to give it away in the form of a necklace . . ."

"It is wrong," Mr. Roma said. "I feel in-

106

side that it is wrong."

"You're getting as full of hunches and superstitions as Carmelita."

The words written on the floor were becoming clearer. "Luisa might think that the necklace is a payment of some kind."

"Then she's very silly. There's nothing I'd want to buy from her. I told her — I merely *asked* her to be a little discreet about what she said to the Banners. It's none of their business, about John and Billy. It might actually upset them," she said earnestly. "You see? It's for everybody's good, really."

"I see."

"It would be tragic for poor Luisa to have to give the necklace back now. She's crazy about it."

The victory was hers. He could force Luisa to return the necklace, but he knew that the necklace itself was no longer important; the real issue was the power Mrs. Wakefield had given to Luisa. By urging her to be discreet she had put into her hands the weapon of indiscretion. Luisa's power would only be reinforced and sharpened by resentment over the loss of the necklace.

"I will not ask her to give it back," he said.

"I'm glad you've seen it my way."

"I *don't* see it your way, Mrs. Wakefield. I know there is nothing to be done, that is all."

She went out of the room without answering. A few minutes later he saw her crossing the lawn, wearing a terry cloth robe over her bathing suit and carrying a face glass and a pair of rubber swim fins. Before she turned onto the path he had a sudden glimpse of her face; she looked as if she was going to retch.

She has courage, he thought, to go into the sea again.

Jessie was lying on her stomach on the big rock gazing down into a tide pool, absorbed in the strange tiny world uncovered by the ebbing tide. In this world anything was possible. A queen fairy was curled up asleep on a pebble, and a castle grew upside down in a forest of flowers. When she leaned way over to touch one of the flowers with her finger it squeezed itself shut till it looked like a brown stone. These fierce flowers had a wonderful name — Jessie called them Sea Enemies, and sometimes at night when she was compelled to frighten herself in order to stay awake longer, she pictured the Enemies waiting very quietly in the pool to eat her arm off.

"Hello," Mrs. Wakefield said.

Jessie rolled over on her back and sat up. "Hello."

"I thought Luisa was down here watching you."

"She went away. We had a fight. Not really a fight, though. I didn't scratch or bite her," Jessie said virtuously. "*Or* pinch."

"I couldn't imagine you pinching anyone."

"I often have. But I think I'm going to give it up from now on."

"Here. I'll lift you down."

"No, thank you." She slid off the rock backwards and landed in the sand with a neat somersault. The exhibition cost her several new scratches on her arms and legs, but it was worth it to see the surprised admiration on Mrs. Wakefield's face. "I looked where you told me but I didn't find any starfish. I found a crab and put him inside my bathing suit but he tickled too much. I abandoned him."

"We'll find a starfish, don't worry."

Mrs. Wakefield took off her robe and tied her hair back with a ribbon. "I haven't been swimming for a long time."

"How long?"

"Over a year."

"Are you scared you've forgot how?"

"No."

"You look scared."

"Do I?" Mrs. Wakefield said brightly.

109

"I'm not, though. I know this part of the sea well. It's like my garden, you see? I know what is planted here, and where each rock is, and the best paths to swim along. And, as in a garden, there are things to be avoided. On a calm day like this the stingrays like to browse around in the shallow water. We must be careful to let them know we're coming so they'll go away."

"I could shout."

"There's a better way."

Mrs. Wakefield took Jessie's hand and together they waded slowly into the cold water, stirring it up carefully before each step. The waves slapped Jessie's stomach and stung the scratches on her legs, but she was too excited to feel the hurt.

They moved as cautiously as thieves into Mrs. Wakefield's dark garden where all the flowers were alive and the vines of kelp twined around Jessie's legs like ivy seeking a wall to grow on.

Mrs. Wakefield lifted a strand of kelp and put it around Jessie's neck. "See now, you have a *lei*."

The leaves of the kelp felt cold and oily against her skin. She said, shivering, "I'd just as soon not have."

"All right." Mrs. Wakefield threw the kelp back into the water and it drifted slowly away. "There's nothing to be afraid of, Jessie."

"I'm not afraid of *anything!*" Letting go of Mrs. Wakefield's hand she flung herself forward into the water, shrieking, "I can swim! Look, I can swim!"

The next wave caught her and she rolled into shore like a log.

Mrs. Wakefield stood motionless, rooted in her garden. It was as if time, and herself, had been paralyzed, and she must stand forever watching a scene that she had watched before, hearing the same sounds. The water crashed against her thighs, a gull cried, childlike, the sun was bright as a devil's eye. From its ledge the black flash of a cormorant swooped out to sea. Jessie sat up, gasping and rubbing her eyes. Mrs. Wakefield looked up at the house which peered slyly over the cliff like a knowing face.

9

"Billy?"

Her own voice came up through the years, trailing moments that had been, not lost, but waiting in ambush for her return.

"Be a good boy now and answer me, Billy. You're not hiding again, are you?"

Sometimes when he was hidden he gave himself away by answering, or by giggling with delight at having fooled her.

She went through the house calling him, very softly, so that she wouldn't disturb Miss Lewis. It was Miss Lewis's day off and she was still asleep in the room above Billy's. Miss Lewis could awaken at the drop of a pin, and she went to sleep just as readily, anywhere and any time, as if her whole body had been trained to respond to the closing and opening of her eyelids. I close my eyes, I sleep. I open my eyes and I am instantly alert, ready for activity, competition, disaster, death, or just a sunny day.

"Billy . . ." The word crept through the house like smoke, and Miss Lewis sat up in bed, scratching the thinning hair above her left temple. Nine o'clock, a sunny day. Too fine to be wasted.

She began to dress, knowing that it would be only a matter of time before Mrs. Wakefield appeared, in need of help. Whenever Billy disappeared for a few minutes Mrs. Wakefield became very perturbed. She didn't show it by wringing her hands and getting all excited, but she got what Miss Lewis described to herself as a "gone" look on her face. Mrs. Wakefield never seemed to realize that Billy always turned up, in the toy chest in his room, behind the davenport, or in the broom closet. Hiding was Billy's favorite game, and when Miss Lewis found him he always looked so comically pleased that she couldn't help laughing.

Miss Lewis had known other children like Billy and she had never been repelled by their appearance the way many people were. She considered Billy rather appealing, with his expression of vivacious curiosity and his button nose slightly pink at the tip, like a clown's.

A sunny day.

Miss Lewis pulled aside the drapes, squinting under the sudden splash of sun. When she picked up the brush and began to do her hair, her glance into the mirror on the dressing table was impersonal and uncritical, as if she was meeting a new patient for the first time and was reserving judgment.

"Billy . . . Now answer me, be a good boy, Billy. Are you hiding?"

Of course he's hiding, Miss Lewis answered silently through the closed door. Under the flying brush her hair sparkled with electricity; it stood way out from her head, a nimbus of fine gray wire.

Of course Billy was hiding. She should *know* by this time. Always getting in a tizzy. A very quiet tizzy, worse, in a way, than the screaming-meemy kind. Emotional, oh my, yes, in spite of that firm controlled manner of hers. Emotions were necessary, Miss Lewis conceded that, but she kept her own, as she kept her best gloves and handkerchiefs, in an old chocolate box covered with a sachet of rose petals.

"Coming," she said briskly, like a general with fresh troops and supplies coming in to replace a battered and defeated division.

She opened the door and Mrs. Wakefield said, looking quite "gone": "I'm sorry I woke you up."

"I'm not much of a one for lying in bed," Miss Lewis said, rebuking the defeated troops who might easily have lost the battle by lying too long abed, or having unboxed emotions. "I heard you calling. Now you know, you *know*, he *likes* to be called. Remember the time he was in the broom closet? Hours, it was. Simply because everyone made such a fuss calling him."

"He — he never used to hide like this."

"It's only a new game he has. I'm rather pleased with it myself. It shows a development, a step forward. He's getting more independent. Look at it that way."

"I'm afraid he might hurt himself."

"He hasn't yet," said Miss Lewis. Afraid. Yes, that was the word for Mrs. Wakefield's expression, not "gone." A constant fear that fitted as tight as her skin.

Miss Lewis felt a sharp little pain in her chest, invisible under the starched chambray house dress — a twitch of revelation. Was Mrs. Wakefield's fear merely that Billy would hurt himself, or was it much deeper, uglier: *I am afraid because in the very bottom of my mind, in the depths where I live naked and absolutely alone with myself, Billy is dead, drowned, never existed.*

If such a fear existed, Miss Lewis knew that no one could ever find out — except in terms of results — least of all, Mrs. Wakefield herself. She could never recognize it because it was already broken up into little digestible chunks. It was natural, even commendable, for a mother to be afraid that her son might hurt himself. A cut, a scratch, a fall, these were legitimate worries, viewed separately. But when Miss Lewis thought of them as pieces off the big fear, she got a crawly sensation along her spine.

Miss Lewis said, gently, as if in apology for her thoughts, "Have you looked under the beds?"

"Yes. Everywhere I could think of."

"He might be with Mr. Roma and Carmelita."

"No, they're working in the garden."

"Where did you see him last?"

"He was playing with his blocks on the patio," Mrs. Wakefield said. "He was very quiet. I thought I'd run upstairs and change into a lighter dress."

"That's probably just the chance he was waiting for, blocks or no blocks." There was no rebuke in Miss Lewis's voice; she seemed secretly amused that Billy had had wits enough to slip away from his mother and hide. Billy had been showing a great improvement lately, and while Miss Lewis gave most of the credit to the thyroid extract, she took some for herself. The odd part of it was that neither Mr. nor Mrs. Wakefield noticed or commented on his improvement. It was as if they dared not look, or hope, for fear he would slide back again.

"He's getting sharp as a fox," Miss Lewis said.

They went through the whole house again, systematically, so that Billy wouldn't have an opportunity to slip from one room to another to elude them. Miss Lewis found a button that had been missing from her best crepe dress, but no Billy.

"He might be with his father," she said. "Why didn't we think of that before, my goodness."

"John's on the beach. He knows I don't allow Billy down there without me. It's too dangerous."

"We'll have a look anyway."

They crossed the lawn, fringed satin embroidered with clumps of marguerites. It had rained during the week. The trellis beyond the patio was a wall of white and scarlet and mauve sweet peas. The ribbed leaves of the loquat almost hid the golden eggs of fruit. The oleanders were choked with blossoms, and the camellia tree stood like a duchess, pink and perfect after its bath.

"It's a pity they don't smell," Miss Lewis said. "The camellias." But she sniffed them anyway as she passed, just to make sure.

The sun was steaming off the moisture from the roof of the house and from the boulders at the top of the cliff. In the windless air the steam rose straight and purposeful, as if to complete the cycle of change without delay: the cloud, the rain, the steam, the cloud.

Shielding her eyes from the sun, Miss Lewis knelt at the cliff's edge and peered over at the stretch of sand below.

"Of course. Just as I thought. He's with his father, you see?"

"Yes." Mrs. Wakefield knelt too, looking a little humble, as if she were kneeling not only to see over the cliff more easily, but out of gratitude to a nameless and unpredictable god.

"There now," Miss Lewis said crisply. "He's perfectly all right. Better not lean on that boulder. It's a little unsteady, I noticed the other day."

"It's time," Mrs. Wakefield said, "time for Billy's orange juice."

"It won't hurt to wait a bit. But I'll bring him up if you want me to."

"It's dangerous down there," Mrs. Wakefield said vaguely. "The tide, rocks — really dangerous."

"I'll fetch him."

"Yes."

Miss Lewis's retreating footsteps beat in her ears like the pulse of the earth.

Below the cliff, the father and the son. Their voices rose straight as the steam, but already dissolved before they reached her, already turned into something else in the cycle of change.

"See, Billy? It's fine, isn't it? Dip your feet in, feel it. Isn't it nice? Take my hand. There, now. You must *try*, Billy, try very hard. You're getting to be a big boy."

He was a big boy, but he hung back, burying his face against his father's ribs.

"We'll surprise your mother, won't we? She'll be flabbergasted when she finds out you can paddle and float around and perhaps even swim eventually. Wouldn't you like to surprise her, Billy?"

Yes, yes, but there must be other ways besides the cold and terrifying water. To hide and be found, to have a bowel movement at the right time, to clean his plate, to build a tower of blocks — other ways, soft as hair, warm as cocoa.

"You must *try*, Billy."

Yes, yes. He moved his head up and down against his father's ribs, willing to try, willing to surprise, yes. But the waves were animals with cold wet mouths.

John and Billy, turned to gold in the sun, advancing into a molten blue mirror that absorbed their golden skin inch by inch.

Wait, Mrs. Wakefield thought, *wait for me. We will all take a walk in the sea, my garden. We must stay together, the three of us. Wait for me.*

Into the garden, the mirror, the cold wet mouth.

"That's my big boy. Now isn't it fun? It's like having a bath."

Yes, but the tub was enormous as eternity, the water icy as death, and Miss Lewis was not there with her steamy hair and soft, soapy hands. Miss Lewis, Miss Lewis!

"You can splash all you want to. See? You splash me first, Billy. Go ahead, splash me, Billy."

I cannot.

He pushed away, butting his father with his head, goatlike. He tried to run but the water was heavy, it dragged at his legs and pulled them down, it tossed him into a ball and chased the ball shoreward.

In the safe sand he uncurled like a giant worm, slow and silent, while Mrs. Wakefield's scream ricocheted against the cliff wall.

Miss Lewis picked him up, pressing his dripping head against her starched chambray bosom, soothing him not with words but with low crooning sounds that she had learned a thousand years ago and had never quite forgotten.

Staggering under his weight she carried him up to the drier sand already hot with sun. He liked to be carried, to swing in time to Miss Lewis' body and feel her warm quick breathing against his neck. He cried when she put him down, and lifted his arms to her like a baby. But in a moment he forgot what he was crying about. The tears dried on his cheeks leaving freckles of salt.

With Miss Lewis beside him he felt safe again, and pleasantly excited at her funny noises and at the sight of his mother scrambling down the face of the cliff calling his name. It was better than hiding and being found.

He felt quite safe again, yes, but he wasn't ready yet to look at his father coming out of the jaws of the sea.

"He's all right," Miss Lewis said. "He's a big brave boy. And he fooled us, didn't you, Billy? We didn't have any idea you were down here, swimming. My goodness!"

He had surprised them, after all. Miss Lewis trembled with surprise, and his mother was paper-white; and even his father, who had arranged the surprise, seemed quite taken in by it.

Everything dripped; his own hair, his father's swimming trunks, his mother's eyes. So much dripping, he urinated in the soft sand.

"Let's go put on some dry clothes," Miss

Lewis said. "Come along."

He lifted his arms to be carried, but she said, half-laughing: "You're too heavy, Billy-my-boy. You weigh a ton."

"I'll carry him up," Mr. Wakefield said.

Billy shook his head, grabbing at Miss Lewis' skirt so that she almost fell. She helped him to his feet and they went off together, hand in hand, with Miss Lewis talking a blue streak.

Mr. Wakefield looked after them, defeated, shivering, feeling on his back and shoulders not the heat of the sun but the cold eyes of conscience.

"He let go so suddenly," he said at last. "He made a push and knocked my breath out before I had any idea what he was going to do."

"You shouldn't have brought him down here at all."

"He isn't hurt."

"He might have been. I'm not blaming you, I'm not. I was watching. I know how it happened. John . . ." Billy and Miss Lewis were at the stone steps now, and she was showing him how to hold on to the guard rail. From a distance they both looked very tiny and vulnerable, breakable dolls. "John, don't ever bring him down here again, promise."

"I thought he'd enjoy it. I thought — well, he seemed so much better, almost — almost normal. I thought you'd be — pleasantly surprised if I . . ." His voice dissolved at the base of his throat, and crystallized further down, thin and brittle as glass. "Miss Lewis said he showed a definite improvement. I wanted to — well, to enlarge his experience. I — expected too much of him, I guess. I'm sorry."

"You must promise."

"Yes. Yes, I promise."

He felt sometimes that he lived within walls of promises and couldn't breathe; a prison of promises. Promise me that you will never send him away to a school or anything. Promise that we will keep him with us always, away from other people, just with us so he'll never know he's different. Promise to make it up to him that he was ever born. Promise patience, faith, restraint, love, charity, strength, pity. Promise promises.

He turned to look at her and he saw that she was suffering more than he was. It was out of her womb that Billy had come, her son, her freak. Freak freak. He stabbed the word viciously into his heart, and pulled it out, and stabbed it in again until it was softened by his own blood.

It was no one's fault, not his or hers or

some obscure great-great-grandfather's. It was an act of God. No blame could be apportioned, no justice expected.

"John." Her hand was warm on his arm. "John, sometimes you look as if you hate me."

"Hate you? I could never hate you, darling."

It was true. He would always love her, it was the only promise in the wall that couldn't be pried loose, or fall out from decay.

A gull cried, childlike, the sun was sharp as a devil's eye. From its ledge the black flash of a cormorant swooped out to sea.

10

They found the starfish clinging to the underside of a rock in the shallow water. Mrs. Wakefield saw it first, just the tip of one of its arms uncovered by the ebb of a wave, but she said:

"You'd better investigate that rock, Jessie. I don't seem to be able to find a thing."

And so Jessie discovered the starfish for herself, and it was, from the first, her very own. It wasn't as sweet and delicate as the baby one but it was far more sumptuous. Its five arms were fat and strong, violet-blue studded with silver beads. It was as big as Mr. Roma had promised it would be — as big as her head — and it clutched the palms of her hands powerfully, and curled one of its arms in dignified outrage.

"Look-it," she cried in ecstasy. "He thinks I'm a rock, look-it!" And indeed, she felt like a rock, a fortress; a protector of all starfish; their friend, Jessie Banner.

"He can't really think at all," Mrs. Wakefield said.

"A little bit."

"No, not even a little bit."

"But he must!" It was monstrous that he could be so alive and beautiful and not be able to think, to know he was with a friend.

"He can't feel either. At least, very little."

"He can feel me. He is doing it right now."

"Yes, but he can't feel the way we do. If we cut off his arm he wouldn't mind very much. He'd just go ahead and grow another one."

"He can feel *me*," Jessie repeated stubbornly.

"He won't feel it when he dies, that is what I meant." Mrs. Wakefield took the starfish and laid it flat on her palm, straightening out the curled arm. "Starfish aren't like us, Jessie. They are hardly alive at all. They can't even make a noise."

"Does he have to die?"

"We all do, some time."

"Not little *girls*, though?" Jessie said. Old people, yes, and very old dogs with no teeth; house flies, and bees that had lost their stingers, people who caught dreadful germs by not washing their hands before meals, fish on a hook, and elderly horses gone blind and deaf, and even little boys who couldn't swim. But not little girls.

"Not little girls," Mrs. Wakefield said.

"Naturally not." She'd known it all the time, of course, but it was pleasant to be reassured. She said soberly, "If he's going to die I don't think I'll name him. I have about a hundred names ready, though. I've got to save some of them for when I have children and puppies and kittens and rabbits, but I could spare one."

"No, we won't name him."

The starfish, anonymous, mute, without thought or feeling, was carried up to the kitchen where Mrs. Wakefield filled Carmelita's spaghetti-boiling pan with water and put it on the stove.

The starfish sat quietly on a newspaper on the floor with one arm raised tentatively like a shy child in a classroom.

Standing on a stool beside the stove Jessie looked down into the water and watched it get warmer and warmer, until it began to swirl in the pan and the steam rose, dampening her brows and lashes, giving her a moist, beady little mustache.

The steam didn't smell exactly like steam. Even though the starfish hadn't yet touched the water the steam that curled through the kitchen was subtly tainted with the smell of fish.

Carmelita noticed it, too.

"Such stinks," she said, holding her nose and indicating her great anguish. "All over the house it'll be stinks, stinks."

"Nonsense," Mrs. Wakefield replied in Spanish. "It won't smell at all. I've done this many times."

"Already I smell it."

"It's your imagination."

"My casserole, and now my spaghetti-pan. Pretty soon I'll have nothing left, and we'll be living on baked potatoes. Nothing but baked potatoes, morning, noon and night."

"I like baked potatoes," Mrs. Wakefield said calmly. "They're very nourishing."

"She talks funny," Jessie observed. "Why doesn't she talk like us?"

"She could if she wanted to, but she's a very obstinate woman."

Carmelita denied this by stamping to the door. She stood on the porch sniffing the fresh air with exaggerated relief.

Jessie climbed down from the stool, somewhat dizzy from watching the lively water. She wasn't sure why the water was being heated; she thought it might be to give the starfish a good warm bath to clean him off.

"It's warm enough now for a bath."

"It has to be boiling."

"Boiling is very *hot*," Jessie said anxiously. "He'll burn."

"He can't feel, Jessie, I told you that. And he has to be — fixed, if you're going to keep him. We must boil him for a few minutes and then let him dry out in the sun. After that we'll paint him with formaldehyde and sun him a bit more and then he'll be all ready, very light and strong, yours for keeps."

"But he won't be able to *move*."

"No, of course not."

Hers for keeps, but dead.

The steam rose, a shroud of chiffon, smelling of death.

Mrs. Wakefield bent over the starfish and pressed its upraised arm flat against the newspaper.

"We want him to be a perfect star," she said. "It will be too late to straighten him out after he's boiled."

Jessie averted her eyes. She felt somehow that it was too late to straighten anything out, ever again. She had been trapped by her own words: I want a starfish. Between the wanting and the getting was this room, this steaming witch's cauldron and the witch herself.

Mrs. Wakefield picked the starfish up from the newspaper and slid it off the palm of her hand into the boiling water.

Jessie held her breath tight and hard in her chest, expecting a cry, a protest. At this moment of death the mute might cry out in horror, the insentient suffer, the thoughtless understand.

The starfish sank quietly into the bubbles, to be Jessie's for keeps. There was no cry; only a sudden shocking change of color. The blue arms burst into a new vivid orange-red life, the color of the setting sun.

"Ten minutes," said the witch, "will be enough."

Jessie let out her breath and it left a hollow of pain inside her. She felt quite hollow all over, not a rock or a fortress any longer, but something brittle, filled with fish-scented steam.

"I think I'll go outside," she said, rather coldly.

On the porch steps she sat close beside Carmelita who was warm and brown as a baked apple.

"Esstinks," said Carmelita.

Carmelita's skin smelled ripe. The flies sat on her forehead and her arms and her legs, so that she was dotted with extra little black eyes that could see everything.

"Baby," she said, sighing, patting Jessie's yellow hair. "Hi, baby."

She had wanted many children, all kinds and colors, pale blonde children and red-headed ones with freckles, and dark striking children, but the Blessed Virgin had refused.

She brushed away her extra eyes and fanned herself with her apron.

"You're nice and fat," Jessie said gravely.

Carmelita laughed, throwing back her head and showing all her teeth, white as chalk. Jessie laughed too, until the tears came in silver worms tickling her cheeks.

For the rest of the morning she laughed quite desperately and suddenly at every little thing. Her father, sitting on the patio with his legs angled, was a hilarious frogman. Luisa, with her hair upswept, had a pointed head. Mr. Roma was a forbidden word, a nigger. Yes, a nigger, nigger, nigger. Everything was a scream.

Except her mother.

"What's got into you?" Evelyn asked when Jessie flung herself half-exhausted, on the davenport.

"Nothing."

"You haven t done anything naughty, have you?"

Jessie's face worked; she wanted to tell her mother about the starfish but she couldn't get a grasp on the right words, they slipped away, fishlike, as soon as she caught one. *I am guilty. I have murdered.*

"I hope we're not going to have any scene," her mother said in a warning tone. "Especially after Mrs. Wakefield went to all that trouble to fix the nice starfish for you."

Evelyn put out her hand, as if coaxing her to be less difficult to understand, but Jessie drew away, shaking with inverted tears. Mrs. Wakefield was a red-headed witch, and Mr. Roma was a nigger.

"Stop that, Jessie,"

"Everything is — so — so-f-unny."

"I don't like it when you make those forced-laugh sounds. Now calm down and behave yourself. Why are you sticking around the house like this anyway? Why don't you go outside and play?"

It was simply excruciating to picture herself stuck to the house with glue. She ached all over with laughing and her eyes were so hot and puffed they seemed ready to burst.

The laughter was a cry for help, but no help came.

"If you keep this up you'll go straight to your room," Evelyn said. "And stay there. Do you hear?"

She heard. She ran out of the house leaving a trail of hiccups that hung in the air like bubbles.

Sitting in the sun on a packing case was the starfish, but she didn't look at it. She kept her head turned away and walked past the starfish sideways like a crab.

Starfish, old men, stingerless bees and

little boys who couldn't swim. But not little girls.

Not little girls. The words were a stone fence behind which she would live forever, always young. But the moment had come when she was big enough to see over the fence, and what she saw was, yes, little girls, too.

She saw Jessie Banner in a rolling field of little girls. They lay like flowers dropped into the grass. Drowned, frozen, swatted like flies, slapped like mosquitoes, burned, smothered, broken, left to dry in the sun. She saw herself, Jessie, walking into the field of little girls to share death.

But the vision beyond the fence was too massive; it fell of its own weight into the bottom of her mind like a stone in a pond, and the only clues to its existence were the molecules it displaced, the bubbles of laughter, the hiccups, the swollen eyes.

"Hold your breath and swallow nine times," Luisa said, dreaming on the swing in the pepper tree.

"What will I swallow?"

"Spit," Luisa said. "Imagine, crying, at your age."

"I wasn't crying. I was laughing."

It was very difficult to get enough spit for nine swallows but she did it by pretending she was sucking a lemon.

The hiccups went away and the world was suddenly and beautifully ordinary again. The rope of the swing scraped on bark, Luisa was patronizing and cross, the hummingbirds darted crazily in and out of the eucalyptus leaves and flung themselves at Jessie's head. Spiders took a stroll in the sun and ants marched up and down the pepper tree.

Everything was alive, everything moved and felt and thought. Jessie's pulse beat with love for this ordinary world. She loved even Luisa.

"I don't think you're a stinker," Jessie said.

11

Back and forth Luisa swung and the topaz necklace swung too, against her throat.

She couldn't keep her hands off it; she fingered it like a rosary, and by its divine power she became a beautiful girl with yellow hair singing into a microphone. All the men crowded around her, and even the orchestra stopped playing to hear her better. The throbbing voice went on alone. Among the men was one in particular, the richest handsomest man in the world, swooning at her feet: Luisa, look at me, Luisa, just a glance, don't be cold to me, Luisa! Slowly, contemptuously, she turned her head . . .

"You look funny," Jessie said. "Why are you going like that for?"

"Stop interrupting me."

"You weren't doing anything much."

"I was, I was!" She closed her eyes, but the rich handsome man couldn't be resurrected. "I never have a minute's peace."

"Luisa . . ."

"Now what do you want?"

"I could trade you something for the necklace."

"You haven't got anything valuable enough."

"I have so. It's a secret. No one knows but me."

"How much did it cost?"

"I don't know, but it's gold. It's real gold. Probably cost a million dollars," Jessie said recklessly.

"Then why don't you sell it and buy a hundred necklaces?"

"Maybe not a *million* dollars."

"Let me see it if it's so valuable."

Jessie hesitated. "Promise on your brother's blood not to tell anybody?"

"Sure."

"It's in my room."

"I wouldn't trade the necklace for anything, but I'll *look* at your whatever-it-is." There was always the faintest, vaguest possibility that Jessie was telling the truth and that she had found something worth a million dollars. Not gold, but maybe radium.

Of course it was radium. What else? Jessie had been prying into things as usual and, by a miraculous accident, she'd found a piece of radium on the ground.

On the track of the radium Luisa became quite animated. She skipped along the path behind Jessie, a rich girl, an heiress, courted by dukes, riding to hounds, flying her own plane . . .

"Oh, my God," Luisa said bleakly, and dropped onto Jessie's bed as if she'd been struck from behind. "It's only a *watch*."

An ordinary man's pocket watch with the crystal smashed and the gold chain clogged with dirt.

"But it's gold," Jessie said, "and it really works. It tells the time."

She wound the watch, and sure enough it told the time quite loudly, tick-tick-tick. It was difficult to see the hands through the shattered crystal, but it was enough for Jessie to know that they were there. What time the hands told didn't matter; it was time itself ticking away that was important. Jessie held in her palm the minutes and the years.

Luisa groaned and rolled her eyes. "A lousy old watch. Honestly. Where'd you get it?"

"Somewhere."

"Maybe you stole it, for all I know."

"I never did," Jessie said. "I found it. Finders keepers."

"Let me hold it a minute."

"Why?"

"I want to look at it, is all. I wouldn't trade

for a billion dollars, but I can at least look at it, can't I?"

"It's my secretest treasure and your hands are dirty." She was reluctant to let Luisa take the watch, not because of the dirty hands, but because the watch wasn't entirely her own. She had found it, certainly, and finders were keepers, but her possession of it was, she knew, temporary; it hadn't been ratified by any grown-ups. She had no real hold on the watch, it could be taken away from her at any time and for all sorts of reasons.

Luisa said, cunningly, "Imagine finding a watch on the road."

"Not on the *road.*"

"Where then?"

"You'd tell."

"On my brother's blood I wouldn't tell."

They heard footsteps in the hall and Evelyn came into the room carrying a pile of Jessie's freshly ironed clothes.

"Hi, baby," Evelyn said. She smiled at Jessie and there was a coaxing and uncertain quality in the smile as if she wanted to make something up to her but wasn't sure what it was. Jessie's clothes over her arm were still warm from the iron. The clothes, without Jessie in them, were somehow very sweet; they conjured up a Jessie without faults, a sleeping child, innocent as heaven. It was a shock to come unexpectedly on the real Jessie, looking a little sullen, holding her hands behind her back, her eyes brooding with secrets.

"Open the second drawer, will you, Jess?" she said pleasantly.

Luisa rolled herself off the bed. "I got to be going."

"Don't let me interrupt your plans. I'll just put the clothes away and vanish."

"I got to be going anyway."

With Luisa gone the minutes and the years were very loud in passing. They couldn't be ignored.

"What's the big secret, Jessie?"

"Nothing."

"I hear a clock ticking."

"It's only a watch," Jessie said.

"Daddy's?"

"No one's. Just mine."

"Where would you get a watch?"

"Found it."

"You'd better show it to me, don't you think?"

The moment had come, as she knew it would. That was the terrible part about finding important things — someone else had to lose them first.

She handed the watch to her mother, suddenly feeling almost relieved to be rid of it because it was, in a misty way, connected with the dead man in the woods and the drowned boy.

"It looks quite valuable," Evelyn said. "Where on earth did you find it?"

"Where the birds live in the cliff. I climbed up to see if I could see any baby birds. Not to scare them or take eggs away or anything, just to pat them."

"Now don't get off the track, angel, *please*. All I want is a *straight plain* story."

But to Jessie there was no such thing as a straight plain story. All the details were equally important. How could she describe finding the watch without telling about the baby birds she was looking for, and why, and whether she found them, and how the cormorants kept house?

"They live on fish," Jessie said. "Like eagles. There's a story in a book at school about eagles and their nests weighing a thousand pounds. But not these birds. They just have holes to live in. I didn't find any eggs or babies but I found the watch. There was bird-stuff all over the cliff and on the watch, too. Only I polished it off." She added thoughtfully, "Maybe someone *hid* it there."

"I don't think so. Don't start imagining

things. Someone probably lost it, from the top of the cliff."

"They can't have. I often drop little stones over and they always land at the bottom, on the beach."

Evelyn hesitated, knowing Jessie was right, that the cliff, at the spot where the cormorants lived, was slightly concave. It would be impossible for an object dropped from the top to be caught on one of the ledges.

"I could ask Daddy," Jessie said. "Or Mrs. Wakefield."

"A watch?" Mrs. Wakefield said. "That's odd. No, I know nothing about any watch, nothing . . ."

"What's that in the trunk?"

"Billy's toys and some of his clothes." A linen picture book, a doll with a wooly yellow wig, a teddy bear with one eye and one ear, a striped jersey, a pair of pajamas without a string — Billy's. "I haven't quite decided what to do with them."

You could give them to me, Jessie thought. I could play with them and dress up for fun. But the words remained unspoken; death lay in the folds of the clothes like mothballs.

The trunk gaped at her and suddenly

closed its mouth with a click of teeth. She jumped back, as if the teeth had barely missed catching her hand or her foot.

"I could give some of them to you," Mrs. Wakefield said. "Would you like that?"

"No, thank you," she said faintly. "I give some of my own things away all the time to the people in Europe." She edged away toward the door. "I've got to go now. My mother's waiting."

Mrs. Wakefield locked the trunk. "You tell her — tell her I don't know anything about the watch. As far as I'm concerned you can keep it."

I hate lying to a child, she thought. And yet it's for her sake that I'm lying.

With a sound of mourning she leaned against the trunk. The beat of her heart was loud and hard, as if the heart itself had become an external organ suspended on a chain between her skin and her clothes. She felt weak from the strain of lying, and the sudden shock of seeing the watch again, not in John's pocket, but dangling from Jessie's hand and still ticking. Still ticking after all this time, after the wind and the weather, the sea fogs, the malignant sun.

John had kept it in his pocket, and sometimes Billy sat on his knee and held the watch against his ear, listening to the mystery of the hours, the passing of the minutes that would never pass again.

Billy sat, quiet and heavy, wearing the watch like a golden earring. He had a watch of his own, a fat silver one, and its sound was louder than that of his father's watch, but cold. It was nicer to lean against his father's chest and hear, besides the ticking, the rise and fall of a heart, the faint rumble of a stomach; to smell tobacco and sweat and shaving lotion; to feel tiny wire whiskers that stung when they were touched.

"You'd better get down now, Billy. You're getting awfully heavy. Wait now. Be careful of the watch."

He did not want to leave the warm moving womb of his father's lap, but he was thrust out, into birth. He looked with hate at the hands that pushed him. These hands with the fuzzy yellow hair were hostile. They had pulled him into the jaws of the sea, and now they pushed him away, they tore the watch from his ear. Hate, hate.

"Get down now, Billy. That's a good boy. No, Billy, no! Get down . . . Janet," he said. "Janet help me."

She helped him. The bites on his wrist weren't deep, but they bled inside like a mortal wound.

"John . . ."

"No, I'm all right. I — you'd better take him to his room." She picked Billy up, and he hung in her arms like a sack.

"He didn't mean it, John. You know he didn't mean it."

"Please. Take him away."

She carried him to his room, shielding him with her strong arms. Her baby; a big boy, too heavy to be carried, but still a baby, not knowing what damage he could do.

When she returned she saw the watch lying face down on the rug, still ticking.

"He just doesn't know his own strength, John," she said.

"No."

"Perhaps it's a new phase, part of the improvement Miss Lewis talks about. He could be — well, asserting his independence. He doesn't need us so much any longer."

She thought of a dozen explanations, but she never thought that Billy hated to be born. Brought, reluctant, out of the womb, he could only find his satisfactions in an approximation of it. And, as he grew older, there were less and less of these satisfactions. He was too big to be carried, to sleep with Miss Lewis, to be held long in a lap. More was expected of him and less was given. Time was his enemy. He was eight

144

years old, further and further away from the warm safety, the gentle rocking.

"He could be plain bored," she said. "After all, other children get that way when they're ready to take a new step forward."

"What's the use of talking, of trying to explain things?"

"I only want . . ."

"We can't handle him any more, Janet. He'll have to be sent away to a school."

"No, no! You promised me!"

"It's a promise I can't keep," he said heavily. "We've lived here for a long time now, without friends. I'm beginning to feel — more than lonely, almost a little queer . . . I can't tell you . . ."

"He's our son, we can't send him away. They couldn't understand him as I do. They might be cruel to him."

"Perhaps we're the ones that are cruel." The toothmarks on his wrist were vivid against his bloodless skin. "He seems to hate me lately. And sometimes I feel that — that I'm beginning to hate him in return."

She couldn't breathe for pain. "That's a terrible thing to say."

"Worse to feel," he said. "Much worse." He stooped and picked up the unbroken watch.

"You need a change, John. You could take

a trip. A cruise, perhaps."

But he didn't take a cruise. His departure was a final voyage on an unreturning ship.

Leaning against the trunk she saw, for a moment, the pattern of her life, with the black patches of death sewn in with steel by a steel hand. Though she called it fate, the steel hand was her own.

Outside, Mr. Roma rang the bells for lunch, the silver sleigh bell first, and then the cowbell to summon Jessie and Luisa from the woods.

Mrs. Wakefield dragged herself upright, dreading the questions she might be asked about the watch, already planning answers that seemed reasonable.

But the subject was carefully avoided during the meal, and she wasn't sure whether her lie had been accepted as the truth, or as an excusable lapse in taste, like a belch.

12

Outside Mark's window the swallows fussed in the live oak tree.

"After all, as civilized people we're supposed to be a little tolerant," Mark said. "So she told a lie. What of it?"

"Honestly, darling. I didn't say anything *of* it. I merely mentioned the fact that she was a liar and I wished she'd go away. We don't owe her anything."

"Except the house."

"We're paying for that," Evelyn said. "What's more, I'm not civilized. I'd like to march right up to her and say, come on, cookie, explain yourself."

"You'd like to but you won't."

"Well . . ."

"And maybe she can't explain herself. Did that ever occur to you?"

"She can. Everyone can, up to a point."

"All right. You explain yourself to me up to a point."

Evelyn raised one eyebrow. "I don't consider that very funny."

"I was completely serious."

"I can explain myself very easily, as a matter of fact. It's other people who are complicated. You," she said gloomily, "and Jessie and Mr. Roma, everyone, practically."

Mark smiled. "Me's a little queer. Righto."

"That reminds me, if you're going to go out in that silly rubber raft, you'd better use some suntan oil."

"What's silly about it? It was a bargain. War surplus. Complete with two paddles, twenty-five bucks."

"I thought you bought it for Jessie's birthday."

"I'll get her something else." He stepped into his swimming trunks and pulled the drawstring tight and automatically drew in his stomach.

"You have quite nice legs," Evelyn said thoughtfully.

"All the better to . . ."

"And a vulgar mind."

"Righto again, little mother."

She glanced at him, half-pleased, half-suspicious of his mood. "What's behind all this fine fettle?"

"You." He lifted her off the floor and pressed a kiss on her throat. "You, angel."

"Me and who else?"

"God, here we go again. Hand me the oil, will you?"

"I'll put it on for you."

She smoothed the oil on his shoulders and back. His skin was still peeling a little from his last sunburn, and she touched it very gently.

"Change your mind and come with me," he said.

"No, thanks. You only want me to help with the paddling. Remember last time I went out in a boat with you — at Fire Island? All you did was snarl out orders like Captain Bligh."

"It was windy and we were drifting. Nor did I snarl."

"And Captain Bligh was just a sweet old man, right." She paused. "Why don't you take someone else with you?"

"Such as?"

"Well, Mrs. Wakefield would probably enjoy it." Evelyn's voice was as bland as the oil on her fingertips. "She's a good swimmer too. You wouldn't have to worry about drifting. She could just take the rope between her teeth and swim the boat in."

"Very funny."

"I think so."

"What would you do if I really did ask her?"

"I don't know. Try me."

"I will."

Evelyn's smile was shaky as she screwed the top back on the bottle of oil. "Go ahead."

"I wish I understood you. I know you're jealous of the woman — why needle me into taking her out in a boat?"

"Because I know you want to. I might as well be the one to suggest it, it's easier on my pride."

"I don't want to. I'd rather take you and Jess."

She ignored that. "I feel noble as hell, sending my husband off on the high seas with another woman."

"Listen, Evelyn. If it's going to bother you, I won't go. Let's skip the whole thing."

"I'm not bothered in the least. Honestly." She turned at the doorway. "If you see a hot jealous little face peering at you from the window, it won't be mine."

"Won't it?"

"Have fun."

She went downstairs and sat for a long time in the living room with the drapes closed, wondering why, when she talked to Mark, she used superficial frivolous words that never indicated the storm of passion in her heart.

The air was windless, but out beyond the breakers the swells were long and deep, and the boat rose and fell like a yellow balloon.

"There's a storm somewhere," Mrs. Wakefield said, as if to herself. "Perhaps a thousand miles away, but still we feel it in the swells; the whole sea is disturbed."

The rubber bottom of the boat was thin and pliable. It moved as the sea moved, it breathed under the soles of her bare feet. She stood up, and it was like walking on the water; she felt the storm a thousand miles away with the soles of her feet.

"Sit down," Mark said.

His voice startled her. In the prow of the boat with her back to him, she had almost forgotten he was there.

"Sorry," she said.

"If you're tired of paddling I'll put out the sea-anchor."

"That would be nice."

She sat down facing him, with the paddle across her knees.

He threw out the funnel-shaped piece of canvas to keep the boat from drifting, and in a few minutes the rope tautened and pointed the prow shoreward.

Twenty yards away, on a clump of kelp, a pelican sat, curious and unafraid, eyeing the fat yellow monster with two heads and four arms. The pelican meditated, moving his beak like an aged man chewing his gums. The sea monster did not alarm or surprise him. He was an old bird and knew his enemies.

She would have liked to take the pelican and make it her own, but she knew he was more powerful than she was; and so she shouted at him and waved the paddle to frighten him away.

"Leave him," Mark said. "Pretend he's an albatross."

Her smile was faint, fleeting. "You're not ancient enough to be the mariner." But she put the paddle down again, and the old bird sat ruminating, until the yellow monster drifted slowly away, its four arms quiet.

She couldn't own the pelican, but the storm was hers alone. Sliding under her feet from a thousand miles away, the storm belonged to her; she owned the weather. It was as if no one knew about the storm, or felt it, except herself and Mark, whom she had told. Just the two of them, sharing a secret. . . .

"Your — wife is very sweet," she said, looking a little self-conscious. "It's kind of her to put up with me like this."

"No trouble at all."

"And Jessie — I'd almost forgotten there were children like — like that." She pressed her hand against her forehead. "Really, I think I'm getting a little — seasick."

"We can go back."

"No, not yet. I'll get over it."

"Breathe as deeply as you can."

"I'll try."

She breathed deeply, through her mouth, and her full mature breasts rose and fell. He turned his eyes away, a little disturbed and a little angry at himself too, as if he'd been caught staring down the front of a blouse.

"Feeling better?"

"Yes, thank you. I'd hate to turn back now. I love it out here." Her arm drifted in the water like a pale floating eel. "John and I used to row out here sometimes and dive for lobsters. But Carmelita would never cook them, she thinks they're poisonous unless they come from a fish market or out of a can. So we cooked them ourselves while Carmelita stood around expecting us to drop dead."

"She's a little eccentric," Mark said.

"Oh, no. She merely has convictions."

"That's one way of putting it."

Mrs. Wakefield smiled. "She's a happy woman, though. She has built her own life and she needs no expansion. Not another brick is necessary. Perhaps some day some of it will fall away, like mine, and repairs will have to be done. But meanwhile — meanwhile, she is a happy woman."

"I can't see life as a series of man-made structures. It's fluid."

"No. Rigid and mechanical. Once I thought different, but that was a long time ago. Some of us," she said, "can build like Carmelita. But the rest are like the hermit crabs you see along the shore. They live in one borrowed shell after another."

"And where do you live?"

She turned her eyes toward the cliff. "That's my house up there," she said somberly.

"You built it?"

"John and I together."

"Why? Why there, I mean?"

The question slid off her like oil. "Why anywhere, for that matter? The water's cold out here. Colder than the surf. Are you going in?"

"I'm too comfortable."

"I think I'll try it for a little while."

She pulled the black rubber swim fins over her feet and strapped the face glass around her head. It covered her nose and eyes.

"You look terrible in that get-up," Mark said.

"I know, but I don't care. There's no one to see."

"How about me?"

"You don't have to look."

"I won't."

But he watched her as she slid over the side of the boat into the water. She surface-dived, her fins flicking like a shark's tail. To Mark it seemed a reverse step in evolution, the return of the amphibians to the sea.

When she came back to the surface, he said, "Cold?"

"Paralyzing."

"What do you see?"

"Nothing much, so far."

She submerged again and came up a minute later on the other side of the boat with a sprig of kelp caught in the strap of her bathing-suit.

She stayed in the water for a long time, not swimming on the surface, but continually diving under and coming up for air, as if she was searching for something she had lost.

When she finally climbed back into the boat her lips were blue and her skin rough with cold.

"Did you find it?" he asked.

She pulled off the face glass and rubbed her eyes before she answered: "I wasn't looking for anything."

Briny tears dropped down her face leaving trails of salt.

"What would I be looking for?" she said. "Anyway, the sea's too murky today. I couldn't see anything."

"Here, you'd better put on my sweater."

"I'll get it wet."

"Doesn't matter."

She put his old gray sweater around her shoulders. The color made her look sallow and emphasized the pallor of her full mouth. She didn't seem to care much about her appearance, and it irked Mark a little that she didn't put on some lipstick or comb her hair or indicate, in any of a hundred female ways, that he was a man. The evening before she had been almost coquettish in her eagerness to please. He wondered what had caused the change.

In the west a single cloud rode the sky.

"I hope the storm comes our way," Mrs. Wakefield said. "We've had three dry years in a row now. We couldn't afford to waste any water irrigating, so we kept some of the plants alive by siphoning out the bath-water and the rinse water from the washing Carmelita did. But it was never enough. Only a few things survived. The geraniums — they never give up — and the weeds, of course."

She hesitated, pulling the sweater closer around her. "You asked me a while ago why

156

we wanted to build the house here. There were many reasons, but I think the chief one was the trees. They aren't all wild trees, you know. Many of them were planted there years and years ago by the man who owned the land. It's funny, he had that valuable stretch of coastline, yet he lived all by himself in a shed. The shed is still there. Whenever I look at it I think of the old man living there watching his trees grow, and hoping, as we kept hoping, for a storm to pass this way."

The cloud divided, cut in two by a wind they couldn't feel.

"It's incongruous, isn't it? To have things die for lack of water when the sea is right beside us."

He said, so abruptly that her eyes widened in surprise, "Where do you come from?"

"A place you never heard of. It's just a small town in Nebraska."

"Has it got a name?"

"Of course."

"Why not name it then? You don't have to be cagey. Nobody's going to Nebraska to check up on your past."

"It's very difficult to acquire a past," she said blandly, "in Broken Bow, Nebraska."

"Broken Bow, Nebraska."

"Population, three thousand. On the Burlington line about 200 miles from

Thedford. The home of . . ."

"I get it."

". . . the home of Beeman's Sandwich Bags. I'm thirty-six. I was married eleven years, four months, and three days ago. Before that I taught school in Omaha, which is also in Nebraska, on the Missouri River, population a quarter of a million. The principal industries . . ."

"O.K. O.K."

"Satisfied?"

"Partly."

"You wouldn't like any more straight answers to straight questions?"

"I might. It's a long way out here from Broken Bow, population three thousand, the home of Beeman's Sandwich Bags. What happened along the road?"

She sat in silence for a minute, rubbing the flecks of salt off her forearm.

"I didn't mean to be rude," Mark said in apology. "Maybe that's how it sounded, but I was actually trying to be funny."

"We'd better start back now."

"All right."

"As for what happened along the road, I can't tell you. I don't like revisiting places. I'm not a romantic."

"You're revisiting now."

"Only because I have to."

158

It was strange to Mark that she repudiated the one word that he thought described her. She was a romantic. The rhythm of her voice echoed with lost music, vanished loves and an obbligato of death.

He pulled in the sea anchor and flung it on the bottom of the boat.

He said, "Just what kind of a spot are you in?"

"Trouble, you mean? None. None at all."

"Then what are you covering up?"

"What I choose to."

Unanchored and unguided, the boat was tossing like a cork. Mrs. Wakefield turned around on the seat and picked up the paddle again.

"What side to you want me to paddle on?"

"Whatever you like."

"The left, then."

"Your lie about the watch didn't fool anyone except Jessie," Mark said. "To Jessie anything is possible — you can find a ton of ambergris in the middle of Central Park or a gold watch growing on the side of a cliff."

"The watch belonged to my husband," she said. "I don't know exactly how it got on the cliff."

"You told Jessie she could keep it."

"Yes."

"Why?"

"Children like watches. Anyway, I don't believe in mementoes. They're too painful. I know that the past is dead," she said grimly. "I don't have to keep reminding myself."

"I'm very glad you're not in any kind of trouble."

She shook her head, rejecting the least sign of sympathy. It was the one thing in the world that she knew could break her down; especially sympathy from a man like Mark whose very maleness, powerful and a little rough, made her realize her vulnerability.

"Keep your damned sympathy to yourself."

"As you wish."

A gull circled the boat, squawking. He was young and bold and could outfly the wind.

Mark said, impersonally, "I was hoping we'd catch sight of a sea lion. I heard one last night. It sounded pretty close, though Mr. Roma said there aren't any around here."

"He's mistaken. I heard it too."

"It's a hell of a noise."

"Yes, isn't it? Almost like a woman crying," she added. "Did you ever see a dugong?"

"Not that I know of."

"Sea cows, they're sometimes called. I saw one once, long ago. We were on our honeymoon, John and I, on a cruise. It was at sunrise and the ship was passing an atoll in the South Pacific. We saw the dugong from our porthole. She was sitting on a rock nursing her child. It was terrible, she was so huge and incredibly ugly, yet oddly like a woman, moving her thick lips as if she were talking to the child, and fondling it with her flippers. The child clung to her, unaware of her ugliness or its own."

Sometimes in the night she revisited the rock where the dugong sat with its child, but the child had hands on the ends of its flippers, and it wore Billy's face.

She began to paddle with furious speed, escaping the dugong and its child, the pelican, the arrogant gull, the man in the back of the boat.

Mark didn't try to keep up with her. Partly irritated, partly amused at her sudden haste, he lifted his paddle out of the water. The boat began circling clockwise.

She made a half-turn toward him. "Aren't you supposed to be doing some of the work?"

"I wanted to see where you'd get, all by yourself. You were in such a hurry."

"Now that you've seen, shall we go on?"

"All right."

When they had reached the shore and

pulled the boat up on the sand, Mrs. Wakefield said, "Thank you for the ride. It was very pleasant, in some ways."

"That's good."

"You're really pretty curious about me, aren't you?"

"People as deliberately vague as you are make other people curious, naturally."

"I'll try to be more specific," Mrs. Wakefield said.

"No, don't. I like you the way you are."

Shaking her head, she picked up her fins and face glass from the bottom of the boat and walked away.

"I didn't take a single peek," Evelyn said. "I wish now I had. You're looking quite cross."

"Blow, will you, darling? I want to take a bath."

"Don't I even get a report?"

"Sighted sub, sank same," he said. "No, really there's nothing to report."

"You must have talked."

"Not being mutes, yes, we talked."

She was afraid to ask him any more questions, but she couldn't stop herself. "What about?"

"Dugongs," he said. "Dugongs."

"Is that a joke?"

"No."

"Well," she said painfully. "Some day you'll have to tell me about them."

"Evelyn. For crying in the sink. Listen. You're not jealous of her, are you?"

"Horribly."

"Can't you control yourself?"

"I guess I'll have to," she said. "What are dugongs?"

"Sea cows. Amphibious mammals that give birth to living young."

"She must be pretty fascinating to hold you spellbound for two hours talking about dugongs."

"What do you want me to say . . . ? That she's pretty fascinating? All right. I say it."

"No one could talk about dugongs for two hours except a biologist."

"Other topics were mentioned," he said. "The weather. Pelicans. Broken Bow, Nebraska. The watch Jessie found. She admitted it belonged to her husband."

"Why did she admit it?"

"I told her she wasn't fooling anyone. Now, is the examination over, and what are my marks?"

"A mere pass."

He went into the bathroom and closed the door, and a minute later he was singing in his heavy unmusical bass, "Oh my darling, Clementine."

13

Mrs. Wakefield made no excuses to Mark and Evelyn; she merely sent Luisa with the message that she couldn't have dinner with them. She ate, later, in the kitchen with the Romas.

They drank red wine and hot strong tea, with plenty of tea leaves in each cup so that everyone would have fortunes for Carmelita to tell.

"Money," Carmelita said, loud with wine. "See in my cup, all the money. Ho, I am a millionaire!"

She read all the cups, and they all had money and letters coming, and tall dark men, and trips to far places.

The millionaires sat with their elbows on the table poring over their wealth.

"And the news," Carmelita said. "All good news too, for everyone."

Luisa blinked. "What kind?"

"Whatever kind you want. Yes, it's going to be a good year."

"Oh, it's silly to believe in tea leaves, Mama."

"Your mama *is* silly," Carmelita agreed. For the occasion she had taken the bobby pins out of her hair and brushed it. But the hair was unaccustomed to freedom; it tried wildly to escape her scalp and would not lie down in orderly curls. "It's like a party, except we must do the dishes."

"Luisa will do the dishes," Mr. Roma said.

Luisa let out a bleat. "I can't, I just did my nails. I *can't* put my hands in hot water!"

"Then wash them in cold."

"That wouldn't be sanitary. I mean really, if you ever looked through a microscope the way we do in chemistry class — everything's just crawling with germs. Papa, you simply don't understand about germs."

"I understand about little girls, though."

"You talk fresh to your papa," Carmelita said, "and I will give you a smack on your bottom with the fly-swatter."

"All *right,* but don't say I didn't warn you about the germs."

Luisa did the dishes as she did everything else, with great expression. Fastidiously, she carried them to the sink. Wincing, she rinsed them. Averting her eyes in delicate anguish, she wrapped the garbage. And finally, with an air of sacrifice, she dipped her martyred hands into the hot water.

Now and then her groans penetrated the conversation like the notes of a French horn in a symphony.

"A good year," Mrs. Wakefield said. The inside of her mouth felt limey from the strong tea, but she held out her cup for more. "I'm greedy. I want more letters and trips and good years."

"More men, too," Carmelita said, nudging her tipsily with her elbow. "Eh? More men?"

Mrs. Wakefield tilted the teapot and the liquid flowed out, dark as stout. "No. No men, thank you."

"Ah, but such a waste, a strong finebodied woman like you."

"Lita," said Mr. Roma, "you are getting drunk."

"Then so are you."

"You will be an old wino."

"A wino. Hear that, will you?" She rocked back and forth with indignation, and some of the wine in her glass splashed on her wrists. "Me, an old wino," she said, sucking at her wrists. "All I said was, she will have a good year. All I said . . ."

"What makes a good year, Carmelita?" Mrs. Wakefield asked.

"Him." Carmelita pointed with her thumb at her husband. "Roma. When he is not insulting me."

Mr. Roma grinned self-consciously and reached across the table to pat the back of her hand, still sticky with wine. "That's no answer."

"It is for me. You and Luisa, my baby." She turned to beam at Luisa, who looked back at her with undisguised exasperation. "Isn't she pretty, my little one? And clever. Clever like her poppa. Me, I'm a lucky one, eh?"

"Very lucky," Mrs. Wakefield said. The wine had not affected her, and she felt like someone who'd arrived late at a gay party, a little aloof and disapproving.

"You will be lucky too. Here, drink up. We will see what the leaves say this time. We will make sure."

Mrs. Wakefield drained her cup and left her fortune stranded on the sides.

"Now turn it around three times and make a wish."

"I wish . . ."

"No, you must not tell! Wish only to yourself."

"I can't think of a wish anyway."

"Not any?"

"Only impossible ones."

Carmelita took the cup out of her hands and gazed into it with bleary earnestness. "I see children. A great many children, and they all belong to you. Hoh, you don't believe me? See them for yourself."

The specks of children on the bottom of the cup, larger than the money, smaller than the dark men. "Tea leaves," Mrs. Wakefield said harshly. "Such a fraud. I feel cheated."

She thought of the old gypsy she'd visited when she was Jessie's age — *This child will have a long and happy life.*" She felt cheated, but she would have liked to go on cheating herself: Bring out the cards, Carmelita. Produce your crystal ball, your divining rod, your Geiger counter. Interpret the atoms. Read me the stars.

But the game was over. Abruptly, Carmelita got up and carried the cups to the sink and dropped their fortunes down the drain.

"A cheat," she muttered. "No, no. It is not me who cheats you. You hoard yourself like a miser. You give nothing and take nothing. What a waste!"

"Hush," said Mr. Roma. "Lita."

Mrs. Wakefield stopped him with a gesture. "Let her talk. Let her say what she wants to."

"Carmelita does not mean to be critical. She is upset because she loves you and would like you to have a rich life, a husband, many children."

She felt herself disintegrating under the pressure of their pity. "What a fool I am to

168

come back here and listen to your talk," she cried. "What do you expect me to do — go out and buy me a man so I can have a child? Another child like Billy?"

"Like Jessie," Mr. Roma said. "A little girl, as pretty as you."

"Such a cruel thing to say to me."

Mr. Roma didn't deny it. He merely looked patient, as if he couldn't expect her to understand that cruelty was sometimes necessary. "We must all start over again. These eight years have been like a recess from living, now we must go back, you see? Carmelita and I will open a restaurant. We are afraid of failure, of course, but we are excited by the possibility of success. You, too, must learn to believe in possibilities. The little girl like Jessie — she doesn't exist yet, but she might some day."

She thought of the day she'd seen the dugong on the rock, and of the later time when she was struggling up through the billows of ether. She had a purpose in her mind but the ether clouded it; she couldn't remember . . .

"It's a boy, Mrs. Wakefield."

A boy. That was the purpose. "A boy," she whispered. "Is he — all right? Are his — his legs and arms and eyes — everything all right?"

"Everything's just dandy."

"Where's — John?"

"Mr. Wakefield's just outside, busy thinking up names. He said you were expecting a girl."

"Both . . . Either."

The girls, Miranda, Linda, Harriet, Jane. The boys, William, Eric, Paul, David, Peter.

"I've got a name," she whispered. "William."

"That's nice. A good sound name."

"Billy for when he's — he's little."

"Sure." A pause. "Some of them sure do a lot of gabbing when they're half under. Take over, will you, Hilda? My arms are tired."

New hands pressed hard on her lower abdomen, and a new voice, Hilda's, answered her question:

"You can see Billy later on, when you're feeling better."

She didn't see him that day or the next. The unused milk was pumped out of her breasts and they were bandaged very tight, like the feet of Chinese girl babies, to render them useless.

She smothered her anxiety in questions:

"What color are his eyes, John?"

"Blue. Quite light."

"Which one of us does he look like?"

"Neither."

"I'd like him to look like you."

"No one can really tell yet."

They could tell, of course, immediately. But they didn't tell her for four days, and then no words were used. She held Billy against her dry breasts. He looked like every other Mongolian idiot that she had seen, except that he was her own.

"It's hard to start over," Mr. Roma said. "But you must learn to want things again. Not wanting anything is like being dead."

"I do want things — to be comfortable, well-fed, healthy . . ."

"That's no more than any animal wants."

I want other things too, she thought. A child like Jessie, a man like Mark. She said instead, "What will you do if the restaurant fails?"

"Borrow some money and start again."

"You can always call on me."

"I would prefer not to borrow from any friend."

"A friend," she repeated. "Is that how you think of me?"

"You are our good friend," Mr. Roma said gravely. "We have shared many things together."

Many things, she thought. Many sunsets, many tides; the storms, and the dry years. But in the end they were not friends as he thought. She saw now that theirs had been a friendship of environment. Passing, on a city street, he would be only a colored handyman with a Mexican wife, and she a stranger looking for something she had lost.

Since the day in the hospital when she first held Billy in her arms she had always been searching, without knowing it, for the whole and happy baby whose place Billy had taken. It was this baby which had grown inside her womb. Her belly swelled with it, her breasts ripened; its gentle movements were sweet and mysterious. This, this one was her baby, not the impostor, Billy.

Holding the impostor against her breast, she had screamed in silence and despair: *He's not mine! They've made a mistake. They've mixed the babies up, it often happens, they've given me the wrong one!*

He was hers, though, and after the first terrible moment of denial she grew to love him. But she never forgot the other baby, the one who had lived inside her womb; the child like Jessie.

The door of Jessie's room was half-open, and Mrs. Wakefield spoke softly into the darkness:

"Are you awake, Jessie?"

"Sure."

"It's getting late."

Jessie sighed. Adults were always telling her, in a rather accusing way, that it was getting late, as if they held her personally responsible for the passage of time. "I know. I got my watch under my pillow. I'm pretending it's a cricket."

Mrs. Wakefield sat on the edge of the bed, and held one of Jessie's hands between her own. Jessie's palms were rough with callouses, like a laborer's.

"I used to pretend things like that too, when I was a little girl."

It astonished Jessie that Mrs. Wakefield and Carmelita and her mother had once been little girls, and her father a little boy. She knew it was true, but she couldn't visualize them whittled down to half-size and getting into mischief and acquiring warts.

"Did you get warts?"

"Sometimes."

"Were they charmed away?"

"No. But there was an old Gypsy woman living in our town who charmed things away and told fortunes."

"How?"

"By looking at your hands."

"Did she tell yours?"

"Yes."

"Did it come true?"

"I don't know yet," Mrs. Wakefield said. "Part of it came true, I guess."

"I wish I could have mine told. Can you do it?"

"No."

"You could try," Jessie said hopefully. "You could just *guess*."

"It's awfully late."

"Well, *I* didn't make it late."

"That's right, you didn't," Mrs. Wakefield said, smiling. She switched on the lamp, and sat down on the bed again with Jessie's hand upturned in her own.

"My hands aren't really dirty," Jessie explained. "That's only left-over dirt that got stuck in my callouses and won't come out. To hear my mother talk you'd think I *liked* being dirty, which isn't true."

The sound of the surf in the room was very faint, a distant threat.

"This is the busiest little hand I've ever seen," Mrs. Wakefield said. "Busy hands can't help having some left-over dirt. And look, aren't you lucky? — you've got your initial written right in your skin. See the J right here?"

Sure enough, if you looked terribly hard, you could see a long skinny J with an X on top.

"What does the X mean?"

"Let me think. It could be a kiss, couldn't it? A kiss for Jessie. That's lucky too. I'm sure it means that you will be loved."

"Who by?"

"By the ones you love."

"Just parents and aunts and things like that?"

"Oh no, everyone. Everyone you love will love you."

"Animals, too?"

"Animals, too."

Jessie nodded. "That's nice. Can you see what I'm going to be when I grow up?"

"No, no, I really can't."

"Maybe if I gave you a hint you could see? I'm going to be an A. T."

"A. T. No. I don't . . ."

"It stands for animal trainer. Now can you see?"

"Why, of course!" Mrs. Wakefield exclaimed. "I should have noticed it before. The T's just as plain as day."

It was, too. An enormous T that stood, unmistakably, for Trainer. No A could be found, but that was unimportant.

"Well, that's settled," Jessie said, rather relieved at having her choice of profession confirmed, written, in fact, right into her skin so that her parents could never argue about it and want her to be something terribly common and dull like a pianist or a writer. "Can you see what *kind* of animals?"

"Well, no. I really can't."

"That's all right. I expect it'll be all kinds anyway, starting with little ones and ending up with elephants and eagles."

Mrs. Wakefield laughed. "You're a funny girl, Jessie. How will you train an eagle?"

"I'll get him when he's a baby and look after him and feed him so he'll know I'm his friend. Then I can teach him to carry things, like my dolls."

"You won't have dolls then. You'll be a woman."

Jessie squinted thoughtfully. She couldn't visualize the grown-up and doll-less woman she would be any more than she could visualize the little girl Mrs. Wakefield had been. Time, to Jessie, was malleable. It could be bent and twisted so that she could be a grown woman who trained eagles but still played with her dolls and lived with her parents, and looked the same as she did now except for size.

"I certainly have a nice fortune to look forward to," she said. "And you didn't have to guess at all, did you?"

"No, it's all here, in your hand. It says — it

176

says, this child will have a long and happy life."

The words had picked up echoes through the years, and it was these echoes that Jessie heard, with the sharp intuitive hearing of a child. They were sad words, no matter what they said; they struck mournful bells in her ears.

"But it doesn't *really* say that," Jessie protested.

"Don't you want it to?"

"No." She couldn't explain about the sad words to Mrs. Wakefield; she only knew she didn't want them in her fortune. "You were just guessing then, I bet."

"I was just guessing."

"Then I don't have to count it. I'll count the Animal Trainer and the part about being loved." She took her hand away and hid it under the blanket, as if she was afraid that Mrs. Wakefield would read it too far. Too far and too sad.

Yawning, she lay down. The mournful bells faded, and the watch-cricket began to chirp again under her pillow, quite loudly, so she couldn't be sure that she heard Mrs. Wakefield whisper:

"Good night, Jessie. Good night, my baby."

She felt Mrs. Wakefield's lips touch her

forehead, cool and dry as moths. Jessie murmured, "I love you about ninth-best in the world."

"Thank you, darling."

The light clicked, the dark fell from the ceiling and leaped from the walls.

Good night, my baby. She stepped into the hall and closed the door, and turning, she faced Evelyn. She was half a head taller than Evelyn, but she felt, if only for a moment, unarmed and helpless.

She lowered the lids over her naked eyes.

"I was — was just saying good night to your daughter." She emphasized the last words slightly as if to reassure Evelyn that Jessie still belonged to her, and that she, Mrs. Wakefield, had only borrowed her for awhile.

"She should have been asleep ages ago," Evelyn said.

"She was awake when I went in. I didn't wake her up."

"I didn't think you had, naturally."

Unspoken words hung between them, like poised knives ready to fall.

You want my husband and child.

Yes.

You lost yours, now you must have mine.

Yes. I can't wait for a child like Jessie or a man like Mark. I want your husband and your child.

178

Evelyn said, "If there's anything you'd like, just ask for it."

"There's nothing, thank you."

"Mark's downstairs having a nightcap. Why don't you join him?"

"That's very kind of you, but I was just going to read in bed."

"Well, good night." I hate and fear you, Mrs. Wakefield.

"Good night." I'll fight you, Mrs. Banner.

"See you in the morning," Evelyn said brightly.

14

Toward morning the sea lion moved inshore and cried.

Mark woke at the first sound as if he had been unconsciously waiting for the signal. It wasn't morning yet, but the darkness was graying, and the air in the room felt heavy with moisture.

He pulled aside the drapes and saw that the fog had come in during the night. It floated in wisps through the window, but over the sea it hung thick, smothering the new day and muffling the solitary cry of the sea lion. The sound worried him. It seemed to be a cry for help, and he wondered whether the sea lion was wounded or whether it was looking for its lost young or a straying mate.

Putting on his robe he went out through the French door to the narrow platform built along the second story of the house. The platform served both as a sundeck and as a protection from the heat for the lower rooms. No one used it as a sundeck because one of the arms of the live oak tree had reached out and grown over it, dropping its prickly leaves and stony little acorns at the insistence of the wind. But it was a pleasant place to read in the afternoons or to smoke a final cigarette before going to bed.

The old tree was quiet in the fog, biding its time. It would outlive the drought, defeat the wind, drink the fog. It would not rust, like the iron railing of the deck which was wet to Mark's touch and blistered with rust from the fogs of other years.

The cry of the sea lion hung in the air, trapped in the mist. Mark tried to visualize the sea lion, but the only image his mind evoked was the image of Mrs. Wakefield submerging, coming up, and submerging again with a flick of her black fins.

In the flare of the match Mark's face was melancholy. Somewhere in the invisible sea something alive needed help, something with a heart-beat as strong as his own, and blood as rich. He felt a sense of pity and of kinship with the sea lion that he had never experienced before.

A door opened and shut.

"Mr. Banner?"

He turned, almost expecting to see her wearing her face glass and the grotesque duck's-feet, with her wet hair streaming behind her like eel grass. She came toward

him, her head brushing against the over-
hanging branch of the oak tree. An acorn
fell like a stone, and the leaves rustled resentment.

"You heard it too?" she said hesitantly.

"Yes. It woke me up."

"It *is* a real sea lion then. I thought — Mr.
Roma said that . . . Well, it doesn't matter
now, except I'm glad it's real."

She leaned against the railing, a yard or
more distant from him. But the fog was as
intimate as a sheet, wrapping them together
against the outside world. He could hear
every breath she took, and every rustle of
silk under the polo coat she had belted tight
around her.

"Why are you glad it's real?" he said.

"I can't tell you. You might laugh at me."

"Is it written into the constitution that no
one can laugh at you?"

She raised her chin. "All right, I'll tell you.
Mr. Roma heard the sea lion, only he
thought it was me crying. He thought it was
me crying in a dream. Isn't that funny?"

"Not very. Why did you believe him?"

"Because when I woke up I really had
been crying."

"What about?"

"I can't remember."

In the intimacy of the fog he felt he could

reach over and touch her memory and it would unfold into his hand.

"Could I have a cigarette?" she said.

He gave her one and lit it. "I thought you didn't smoke."

"I don't. Just on special occasions."

"Why is this a special occasion?"

"Oh, the fog, I guess," she said with a vague gesture. "And being up so early, and — oh, everything."

"Am I included in the 'oh, everything'?"

She looked directly at him, and the cigarette glowed in her mouth for an instant like a third and fiery eye. "What do you suppose?"

"I suppose I am. Why did you follow me out here?"

"I couldn't sleep. I heard you come out and I wanted someone to talk to."

"Well, start talking," he said soberly.

"I've — I've forgotten what I was going to say."

"Say anything. I want to hear you talk."

She turned away, shaking her head.

The sea lion began again, and they both looked quickly toward the vanished sea, as if startled but relieved by a sound from the outside world.

"He's at it again," Mark said, the relief evident in his voice. "He might have been injured by a shark."

"Oh, no. He's only playing."

"It's a hell of a time to play."

"He doesn't care. Sea lions are very gay creatures. They like to tease. Once, years ago, John and I tried to catch one, or at least get close to him. He teased us for over an hour, letting us get just so close, and then diving under and coming up a hundred feet away. I could have sworn he was laughing at us. His face didn't change expression but he seemed to be chuckling inside, like a very old and dignified gentleman at the Yale Club looking at the cartoons in *Esquire*."

"I frequently read *Esquire* at the Yale Club."

"Don't tell me things like that about yourself."

"Aren't you interested?"

"Yes, but I don't want to hear them. I don't like to think of you as having — having another life, belonging to clubs and working in an office and going home in the evenings to a family."

"How do you want to think of me?"

"Just the way you are now, standing here, with no background at all."

"I can't stand here forever."

"No. But I wish — I wish you could."

He was silent a moment. The fog had begun to lift, and in the east a faint pink glow announced the coming of the sun.

"I'm beginning to get an idea about you," he said at last. "It's not a nice one."

"Tell me anyway."

"You're going to make trouble for me. Trouble is your middle name."

Her eyes looked huge in the dim light. She pulled her coat collar high on her throat, as if to make it less naked, less vulnerable. "Why do you say that? Why do you look at me like that?"

"I'm catching on. You like to own things, don't you?"

She seemed relieved at his answer. "Oh. Oh, is that all?"

"That's enough. Why are you smiling?"

"I'm happy."

"Are you?"

"I like talking to you, out here in the fog like this. It's much nicer than lying in bed, thinking."

"And crying . . ."

"Sometimes I cry. Not often, any more. It's so useless, and afterwards I can't breathe, and my eyes are swollen."

"I hate to think of you crying."

"You're so funny," she said, smiling. "One minute you're so cynical and hard, the bristling male. And the next minute you're quite gentle."

"Have you never affected other people like that?"

"No."

"Not even your husband?"

"No. John was always gentle."

"Did you own him, too?"

"What — I don't understand."

"I meant, the way you own Roma and his wife. In a quiet ladylike way, of course — pulling the strings so cautiously the marionettes don't jump, they waltz."

She wasn't angry. "That's an absurd idea."

"You own Roma, anyway. You even taught him how to talk. Don't you see how he copies you?"

"I can't help that."

"Tell me, did he change in the year you were away? Did you find him perhaps a little different?"

"Why? I don't see what you're driving at."

"Mice don't always play when the cat's away, but they change. They become a little freer, more relaxed . . ."

"Please don't spoil things," she whispered. "Please, Mark."

"Oh, Christ," he said, and rubbed the side of his jaw impatiently.

The rough scratching sound was pleasant to her. She wondered how sharp his whiskers were and whether they would hurt her skin if he kissed her. But it was almost too late now, and too light. The fog still brooded in the treetops, but the sea was visible, flowing silver in the dawn. She would have liked the fog to come down again like a giant cataract growing over the eye of the sun. She wanted a whole new blind day for herself and Mark.

She stood, shivering. It was almost too late. Mr. Roma would be getting up soon, and Jessie, and Carmelita. Soon every room in the house would be filled with people, or the threat of people. The minutes were bursting like bubbles before her eyes.

"I'd better go in now," she said painfully.

"You'll miss the sunrise."

"I've seen others."

"Maybe this one will be different."

She pulled her coat close around her. "I thought it might be too, for a while. But it's the same old one."

"Don't go in," he said.

They stood at the rusted railing, side by side, and watched the sun climb slowly up the sky. The sea turned rosy, and the head of the sea lion was a black speck, a quarter-mile from shore. He had stopped barking, silenced by the shift from night to day.

"I can't stay here," she said, "and I can't

leave. Do you ever feel like that?"

"I do at this moment."

"It's silly to say now that I wish I'd never met you. But I do wish it, with all my heart. It was only by the merest fluke that I learned you were alive, and now I can never forget it. I feel that I could — I could almost kill you."

"Don't talk like that."

"Not for revenge — only so I wouldn't have to go away from you and keep thinking of you going on as usual without me, reading *Esquire* at the Yale Club. I don't want you to be alive without me."

"Those are funny love words."

"Are they?"

Her hands gripped the railing; they were quite large, and one of the knuckles on her right hand protruded more than the others, as if it had once been broken and had mended crookedly. He took her hand and held the crooked knuckle against his heart.

"I couldn't stand it," she said, "to walk on a city street and always be expecting to meet you; to look up at a plane and wonder if you're in it; to watch every window on a passing train. Are those such funny love words?"

"No."

"When I'm gone will you wonder like that about me? Will you?"

"I don't know. I don't think so."

She tore her hand out of his grasp and backed away from him.

He said, "If you can't bear to hear the truth, don't ask for it."

She spat the word back at him. "Truth!"

"That's it. I'm trying to be honest with you. What do you want . . . ? A couple of quick seductions good for a few tear drops on the pages of your diary? Or do you want to lock me up in your house? Either way, it'll be a first-class mess. Wash the dreams out of your eyes and you'll see it for yourself. I know, I've been in a mess like this before," he said grimly, "and I've learned a little. I nearly lost my family for the sake of a woman whose face I can't even remember any more."

"Can't you?"

"I remember she had three kids."

"And that's all?"

"Yes."

"I hate you," she whispered. "I *hate* you!"

"That's better than watching train windows," he said.

He sounded perfectly under control. But he knew that if she came over and touched him, he would forget his own words and make her forget them too.

She went back into the house, shielding

her crumpling face with her hand.

He smoked another cigarette and watched the sunrise and wondered what would happen if he told Evelyn.

15

He didn't tell Evelyn; he didn't have to. Though she wasn't aware of what had happened on the sundeck, she had read, surely and expertly, the signs of guilt: too much or too little silence, a forced laugh, a shift of glance, a sudden change in an old habit. The last sign was the most striking — for the first time since they'd come here, Mark had shaved and dressed very carefully before breakfast.

She kept the knowledge to herself, letting it grow inside like a tumor hidden, temporarily, under a whole and healthy skin.

During breakfast she was very cheerful, paying special attention to Jessie but not missing a flicker of Mark's eyelids. Mrs. Wakefield had eaten early and had already gone upstairs with her notebook to finish listing the contents of the bedrooms.

"Don't dribble like that, Jessie," Evelyn said. "We don't want the place to be swimming in oatmeal."

"My manners are better when I'm out."

"Well, pretend you're out then. Pretend

you're at — how about Schrafft's?"

Schrafft's was fine. She pretended that she was dining alone at Schrafft's on porridge-sherbet; her mother and father were total strangers, and Luisa, coming in with the coffee, was the cross waitress who wouldn't get a tip.

"Here's the coffee," Luisa announced, as if she had just barely been able to survive the gruelling journey from kitchen to dining room. "Mama says it's terrible this morning because the water's beginning to smell again. We may not have any water at all pretty soon unless it rains."

"I'm sure it will," Evelyn said. "Let's hope so."

"It never rains here in June. Do you want anything else besides the coffee?"

"No, thanks, Luisa."

The cross waitress disappeared, and the total strangers began to talk.

"Mark, did you see that necklace Luisa's wearing?"

"Sorry, I didn't notice."

"It looks like the same one Mrs. Wakefield had on that first day she came."

"Maybe it is. Who cares?"

"I don't actually care, darling," Evelyn said pleasantly, "only it seems odd that she'd let Luisa wear it. It looks rather expensive."

"Mrs. Wakefield *gave* it to her," Jessie said, forgetting she was at Schrafft's. "For keeps."

"You're not making that up, angel?"

Jessie never made anything up, and said as much, with virtuous indignation. "I know for a fact because she *almost* traded it to me for the watch, only not quite."

"In any case," Mark interrupted, "it's not your business, Jessie. It's not ours either, for that matter. Let's drop the subject."

"Well, really," Evelyn said, widening her eyes. "Surely it's a perfectly innocent subject — unless you know more about it than I do?"

"I know nothing about it."

"Then why get so touchy? Jessie, sweet, if you've finished, you may go now."

She hadn't finished, but she rose anyway, and sped for the door. She knew what was coming. The total strangers weren't total strangers any more. They were her mother and father, and they were going to have an argument.

"All right, let's have it," Mark said. "Let the brave front fall and we'll see what's behind it."

"Not a thing."

"That's the way you're going to play it, is it?"

Impulsively she reached out and touched his coat sleeve. "Mark, why do you talk to me lately as if I were your enemy?"

"If I do, then I'm sorry. I apologize."

"What good's an apology? I'd like to know where I stand."

"Where you've stood for the last twelve years. You're my wife, and I wouldn't give you up for all the other women in the country."

She turned away, biting her lip. "Those are nice words, but the way you say them makes me want to bawl."

"You have no reason to bawl, Evelyn," he said quietly. "Perhaps I don't act the dashing lover as well as I did ten years ago, but I do love you. I think you're sweet and bright and amusing, and I couldn't imagine anyone else I'd rather see every day."

"But . . . Now let's have the *but*."

"Can't think of any . . ."

"I can," she said. "*But* along comes a woman like Mrs. Wakefield — or Patty — one of these dreamy June-moon-soon gals who's made a mess out of her life — and what happens? You want to rescue her or make it all up to her or something. And immediately *I* begin to look like something that crawled out from under the floorboards." She hesitated. "Hell, darling, I can be dreamy, too.

June, moon, soon, swoon. See?"

"I've never been unfaithful to you."

"You've come pretty close, though."

"Oh, yes."

"Patty and Mrs. Wakefield?"

"Patty and Mrs. Wakefield. Right."

She was silent for a moment before she let out a queer little cry. "What am I sitting here for? Why don't I *do* something about it? Could I — no, I don't suppose I could."

"Could what?"

"Talk you out of it. You know, sort of analyze her so she won't look quite so good to you."

He smiled, very slightly. "She doesn't look so good to me. You're a funny girl."

"Listen, Mark. Do you really have a crush on her? I mean when you look at her, do you — do you *want* her?"

"No." It was the first lie he told, and he told it as much for her sake as his own.

"You wouldn't admit it anyway."

"Probably not."

She said, after a time, "I wish you weren't so honest. Sometimes I think that people who bend over backward to be honest only do it to be — to be cruel."

"If I lied, though, you'd think up stronger words for me than cruel."

"I guess."

"It's a case of hell if I do and hell if I don't."

She poured his coffee and passed it across the table. "I suppose you think I'm unreasonable?"

"No more than the average woman."

"What would you do if the situation was reversed, and some tall dreamy guy with sideburns came along and decided I was pretty cute."

"Lots of them have, though I can't remember any with sideburns."

"I asked you a serious question."

"Very well. I'd probably ask him to park elsewhere. And if he didn't — and if he wasn't too big — I'd take a poke at him."

"The subtle approach, eh? God, men have simple minds."

"Can you think of something better?"

"I'll try."

He looked faintly irritated. "Don't make a fool of yourself, will you? Don't — humiliate yourself."

"If I don't do it myself, other people might do it for me."

"Listen, Evelyn. Lay off, will you? She's leaving tomorrow anyway. There's not a chance in the world that we'll ever see her again."

But, even as he spoke, the words were incredible to him. It seemed utterly impossible that she would not walk into his life again somewhere.

Evelyn was talking, but the words he heard came from his memory and had been spoken by Mrs. Wakefield: *to walk on a city street and always be expecting to meet you; to look up at a plane and wonder if you're in it; to watch every window on a passing train . . .*

Evelyn found Luisa in the lathhouse beyond the shed. Luisa was sitting on the dusty potting-table, singing to herself. Her voice was full and sweet, like a choir boy's, and when she sang she smiled, pleased at the sound of herself floating out the slatted walls and roof. She sang very loud, to cover the crowing of the rooster in the chicken pen and the ceaseless gossip of the old hens.

In former years the lathhouse had been one of Luisa's favorite places to sit and dream. Then, the air had been heavy with the smell of damp earth, and filled with the expectancy of growth. Seedlings sprouted everywhere, in flats and coldframes and flower pots; the hose dripped, and the earthen floor was cool and moist.

The hose hung now on a nail, unused, in a blur of spider webs. Under the folds of Mrs. Wakefield's old gardening gloves, a black widow slept, in dark innocence. The ground was hard and dry as stone, and the only thing that grew was a stunted pelargonium in a flower pot. Its single bloom matched the color of Luisa's dark-red lips.

In the sterile dryness of the lathhouse Luisa sang. She did not stop when she saw Evelyn. She looked away and finished her sad cheap little song.

"That was pretty," Evelyn said.

Luisa tossed her head, flushing. She didn't want her voice to be called pretty. Terrific, or super, or divine — these were the words that would find an echo in her mind. Pretty was an insult.

She said, "I'm supposed to be practicing."

"I didn't mean to disturb you."

"If I don't keep practicing so Mama can hear me I'll have to go in and do the dishes or something."

It was an invitation to leave, but Evelyn ignored it. Pushing aside a box of withered bulbs, she sat down on the bench along the wall. Dust rose from the bulbs like a sigh.

"Mayn't I listen?" Evelyn said.

"I can't sing if anyone listens. Last year at school I was supposed to be on the Christmas program. I had a costume and everything — an angel costume — only at the last minute I lost my voice. I was scared people would laugh at me."

"Why?"

"I looked so funny. The costume was pure white, and I looked — I looked just like a nigger in it. Angels are supposed to be blond."

"It was silly to feel like that. You have a beautiful complexion. Why, my goodness, other girls your age spend weeks and weeks trying to get a tan like yours."

"It isn't a tan," Luisa said woodenly. "I'm this color all over. I was born with it. In the winter the other girls get white again, and I stay like this." She added, with a sudden frown, "You don't understand. You sort of talk to me like you talk to Jessie. I'm not a child. I'm old enough to get married and have a baby. And if I can't think of any other way, that's what I'll do."

"Any other way to do what?"

"Leave here and go to a city."

"I live in a city. It has its faults."

"At night everything is bright, though," Luisa said. "That's the part I'd like best. And the people. Just think, every time you go outdoors meeting different people and seeing what they wear and everything. Out here, it's gotten so I even appreciate Jessie sometimes."

The roof of the lathhouse was hexagonal,

and the sun, squeezing between the slats, divided Luisa into stripes.

"You'll soon be leaving," Evelyn said. "The house is up for sale."

"No one will buy it when they find out about the water shortage. And even if it is sold I don't believe my father will ever start a restaurant in town. He doesn't know anything about restaurants. All he ever was before was a caretaker." She kicked the leg of the table with her shoe, in quick rhythm, keeping time to the quick rhythm of resentment beating within her. "Maybe we'll end up going away with her."

Evelyn hesitated. She was sorry in advance for what she was going to do, but nothing could have stopped her. She said, "That would be nice, wouldn't it?"

"I'd hate it."

"Why, I thought you and Mrs. Wakefield were old friends. She gave you that gorgeous necklace, didn't she?"

"Only so I wouldn't — only for business reasons."

"Luisa — only so you wouldn't do what?"

"She don't want anyone to know about Billy and Mr. Wakefield."

"What about them?"

"I'm not supposed to tell," Luisa said. "I'm scared to."

"Are you afraid she'll take the necklace away from you? Or worse than that?"

"I don't know. I'm just scared, is all. She gives me the creeps. Billy did, too. I used to have to play with him until Miss Lewis said it wasn't good for me. Miss Lewis was the only one Mrs. Wakefield would listen to. She knew she had to, she'd be sunk without her." She broke off with a sharp sound almost like a laugh. "She didn't fool Miss Lewis or me when she went into that sweet, sympathetic act, the way you were trying to do a minute ago."

"I'm glad I didn't fool you," Evelyn said, rising, and brushing off the back of her skirt. "It was worth trying, though. Maybe some day you'll understand."

"I understand already."

Luisa slid down from the table. She was as tall as Evelyn and as fully developed. The seventeen years that stood between them were like the pleats of a fan that could be folded and unfolded but were always joined at the base.

At the base, they were two women with a common enemy.

"He was funny in the head," Luisa said, fingering the necklace. "Billy, I mean. He was born that way. He couldn't hardly talk, not so anyone could understand much except Mrs. Wakefield, and Miss Lewis. He couldn't even stand up alone until he was over three, and sometimes he just sat for hours with his tongue kind of sticking out. He was awful. I hated to be near him. Miss Lewis didn't mind, though. She used to pet him and call him nicknames like Billy-boy and Old Timer."

Evelyn remembered the first night that Mrs. Wakefield had spoken of Billy: *My son was very of music.... Billy and I were traveling.* ... All the references had seemed to indicate that Billy had been a little different from ordinary sons, a little superior.

"Mr. and Mrs. Wakefield used to fight about him," Luisa said. "Not at first, when he was little; but later, when I got old enough to hang around and listen, I often heard them arguing. Mr. Wakefield always talked quiet, but she used to cry and carry on until he agreed with her."

"What did they argue about?" Evelyn said, feeling, as yet, no pity for Mrs. Wakefield. The boy Billy was still too shadowy; he wasn't a real child who had to be fed and clothed and supervised and given affection.

"Mr. Wakefield wanted her to put Billy in a special school, so then the two of them could go away and live some place like normal people. But she wouldn't leave. All

202

the time she lived here she never went further away than town, and then she was always in such a hurry to get home that she didn't get half the things on the list and my father'd have to go back again next day."

"Did Mr. Wakefield stay here all the time too?"

"No. He had something to do with shipbuilding, and he used to go away sometimes up to San Francisco and Seattle. But this is a funny thing: every time he came home something had happened, like Billy falling and hurting his knee, or Mrs. Wakefield getting an abscess on her tooth, or the filter system breaking down."

The wind slipped through the laths and stirred the dust.

"Every night he was away he sent her a telegram," Luisa said. "She kept them all in the hall desk. When he died she read them all through again and burned them in the incinerator. Before the inquest some men came and poked into everything, even the incinerator, and all of Mr. Wakefield's drawers and his desk."

"What were they looking for?"

"A note. The man said it would make it easier for everyone if they could find a note from Mr. Wakefield saying he was going to kill himself."

"Did they find one?"

"No. There wasn't any."

Through the slits between the laths they saw Mr. Roma coming down the path, carrying the pails of chicken mash. He passed on without a glance into the lathhouse. When he opened the gate of the chicken pen the hens squawked and clucked and took nervous little leaps into the air like fat and ancient ballerinas.

"I better go on with my practicing now," Luisa said, "so they'll hear me."

"I'll go in a minute. What was the result of the inquest?"

"They said he killed himself."

Evelyn said, from the doorway, "Thanks, Luisa. I don't know how it will help, but thank you, anyway."

"I didn't do it for you," Luisa said, frowning. "I did it against her."

"Same difference. You're not frightened any more, are you?"

"Not a bit."

"That's good. After all, she's just an ordinary woman. I expect we're both rather silly to hate her so much. We should feel sorry for her."

She didn't convince Luisa, and she didn't convince herself.

She had now in her possession some of

the facts that Mrs. Wakefield had been trying to hide, but she didn't know how to use them. It would be difficult to admit to Mark that she had pumped the information out of a bewildered adolescent girl. As for the facts themselves, she had no way of knowing how he would react; he might be shocked, or repelled, or his attraction for Mrs. Wakefield might only be strengthened by pity.

It was, finally, Luisa herself who forced the issue.

Luisa perceived in the situation an opportunity to change her role from a common tattletale to a martyr. Taking off the necklace in her room, she saw herself as a pure and nunlike creature kneeling before an altar of truth. She put the necklace in a box left over from Christmas, and gave it to Evelyn to return to Mrs. Wakefield.

She felt delightfully holy for the rest of the morning.

16

The box lay unopened on the bureau where once Miss Lewis had kept her talcum and unscented cologne, and her sterile combs and brushes.

Mrs. Wakefield knew what was inside the box, and she felt no anger at Luisa, only at herself for making an error in judgment. *Poor Luisa,* she thought. *After I leave I'll send the necklace back to her. Perhaps it will be a lesson to her.*

It was two o'clock and she was beginning to feel hungry. She had gone without lunch, partly in order to finish the inventory, and partly to avoid seeing Mark with his family. There was no chance to see him alone, even to say good-bye. Evelyn swept through the house like a wind, penetrating every corner. She dusted and mopped and aired the blankets, singing as she worked, so that there was hardly a moment during the morning that Mrs. Wakefield hadn't heard her voice, or her steps crossing and re-crossing the hall like a patrol.

She packed the notebook, now nearly

half-filled, in her suitcase, and went downstairs to the kitchen.

Mr. Roma was at the sink washing his hands and forearms with a piece of the rocklike soap that he and Carmelita made themselves.

"It is very hot," he said, "considering the morning fog."

Considering the morning fog that should never have lifted. "I haven't eaten. I thought I'd make myself a sandwich."

"There's no chicken paste, the kind you like."

"That's all right."

"If you wanted to wait, though, Mr. Banner could get you some. He is going into town for a haircut."

"When?"

"Very soon, I think."

"Are you going with him?"

"Not today. The pump isn't working so good, I have to see what is the matter."

"I'll ask Mrs. Banner to get the chicken paste," Mrs. Wakefield said. "She's more likely to remember."

"Mrs. Banner is not going either. The jeep is too rough for her."

"Oh."

"I'll tell him to get some then?"

"If it's convenient. I don't want to put him

to any trouble." She paused at the door and said over her shoulder, "I finished the inventory. I think I'll go for a walk."

"A good idea."

"It will be my last walk here," she said with a smile he couldn't understand. "I want to remember every minute of it."

When she went out she saw that the garage hadn't been opened yet, and she knew that if she hurried she would be able to cut through the woods and reach the road in time.

James, the gander, sauntered over with his contemptuous greeting. She passed him without speaking. He was not accustomed to being ignored by people, and he followed her, hissing, and moving his neck back and forth in outrage. The faster she walked, the faster he waddled along behind her, using his powerful wings to gain speed.

She was amused, at first, by the pursuit. But as it was prolonged, past the garage and the cypress windbreak, she began to wonder how far he intended to follow her, and whether his hissing had attracted the attention of the people in the house. She didn't want anyone to know where she was going, and the gander's hissing seemed to point to her and to her destination like a malicious accusing whisper.

She knew how absurd she must look,

racing against time and an obstinate gander. He had never before followed her beyond the garage, and she wondered what perverse devils were driving him.

She stopped, and looked back at him with hatred.

"Go away, James. Go back. Go back now."

She tried to sound patient, in spite of her hurry, but the gander wasn't fooled. He circled her, clockwise, his blind eye, ringed with orange, glowing like an opal. In his male arrogance he thought she was a victim, and when she started on her way again he shortened the distance between them. The flap of his wings frightened the birds. The meadow larks fled to the tree tops and the jays cursed him from the shelter of the leaves.

At the pepper tree where the path curved toward the bridge, she stopped for the second time. Leaning over she picked up a handful of dirt and hurled it at the gander. The dirt hit him square in the face.

He raised his orange beak and honked. The noise was like an earthquake of sound, shaking the trees and splitting the air. Every living thing in the woods responded to the trumpet of war. The lizards streaked for cover. The myopic gophers who had come up to nibble the roots of devil grass, scuttled back into their catacombs, their ears bursting with danger. Every tree quivered with angry birds in ambush.

She waved her arms and shouted. The gander worked the ground with his feet, and raising his bill, trumpeted again.

She couldn't quiet him and she couldn't outrun him. She stood, in despair, expecting that at any moment Luisa or Jessie or someone from the house would come running to investigate the noise. By the time it was explained it would be too late, Mark would already have passed the place on the road where she intended to meet him. It seemed that the whole of nature was in league against her: the morning fog that should never have lifted, the bright day that hid nothing, the tattling birds; everything — time, and the weather, and Mark himself, and the gander's trumpet summoning more of her enemies from the house.

She reached down and picked up a stone.

"Go back," she said, as if the gander was not an animal but a bewitched human who could understand her words. "I warn you, go back."

He honked again, beating his wings powerfully. But he didn't look fierce; instead, he seemed curious, as if he had never before witnessed such strange behavior and was trying his best to do his part in the panto-mime. He had known this silly woman for years; she had fed and watered him and stroked his feathers and chased him away from the chickens; if she wanted now to play a new game, he was willing. He leaped into the air in his excitement and listened to the full satisfying sounds that came from his own throat.

The stone hit him just over his opal eye.

He fell gracefully on his side. His opal eye remained unchanged, but almost immedi-ately a glaze came over the other eye. His legs stuck out from his body, stiff as boards.

He lay among the leaves, looking smaller than he had when he was alive. She came over and spoke his name, "James?" She felt among his feathers for the beat of his heart. There was no blood, no evidence at all to show that the stone had hit him except his instantaneous excretion at the moment of death.

She would have liked to run away and leave him lying where he was; someone would find him and assume he had died naturally, of old age. But she was afraid that the finder might be Jessie. Jessie didn't un-derstand that death could come to her friends.

She decided to carry him further away

from the path and cover him with fallen leaves and branches. There was no way to take hold of him except by his legs. The yellow skin felt like the skin of an old man, dry and cracked. She picked him up very carefully, so the oozing excrement wouldn't soil her dress. He was surprisingly light. His fierce wings and huge body had almost made her forget that he was only a bird, after all; the body was merely fat and feathers, and the bones were like twigs.

Fifty feet from the path there was a small hollow under a eucalyptus tree, which shed its leaves and bark continually. No matter how often the wind swept them away, the ground was constantly littered with chips and chunks of bark. The trunk of the tree, where the bark had already been shed, was as gray and smooth as old bones.

She placed the gander in the hollow and covered him with dried leaves and pieces of bark. His drab feathers were easily camouflaged. When she returned to the path and looked back, she couldn't even see the place where she'd buried him. No one would ever find him. He would lie there until he became part of the earth itself as Billy had become part of the sea. *Not death,* she thought, *only change.* Change, quick and violent and startling, like a hand grabbing you from behind in the dark. It took time to adjust and to realize that, though its pressure was relentless, the hand itself was friendly. *Only change, nothing is wasted.*

She wasn't immediately sorry that she'd killed the gander. Like Billy, like the starfish, it had had no future but death, and that death should have come at her hand (the friendly hand in the dark), wasn't important. She was merely an instrument in the cycle of change. The gander had escaped disease, and the roasting pan, and the wheels of cars, only to die by a stone over his opal eye.

She crossed the barranca, picking her way among the boulders, pursued only by her oven squat black shadow that hid behind the trees and jumped out at her again in the clearing where the swimming pool was, and the old well, gone to salt. A hundred yards beyond, she reached the fence where once a year Mr. Roma posted new No Trespassing signs to replace the ones that had been bleached by the sun or shredded by the wind or turned into a soggy pulp by the sea fogs. She lifted the bottom wire of the barbed-wire fence and crawled underneath. One of the barbs caught the hem of her dress but she jerked free, leaving behind strands of green silk for some enterprising nuthatch to use to decorate his nest.

She sat down by the side of the road, breathing hard and feeling quite faint from the heat.

It was fifteen minutes before she heard the jeep coming along the road. All her worry and haste, the gander's death, the crude burial, had been for nothing. She looked down at the friendly hands that had moved too fast.

It can't have happened, she thought. *When I get back James will be standing under the magnolia tree.*

The jeep came around the curve trailing a cloud of dust.

She stood up, conscious suddenly of the way she would look to him — a woman no longer young, her face flushed and moist, her dress snagged, and her white shoes dappled with dirt. Nervously she smoothed her hair back and wiped off her forehead with a handkerchief.

He pulled up alongside the road.

"What are you doing here?"

"Waiting for you. I thought I'd — drive into town with you."

"You think that's a good idea, do you?"

He was wearing sun glasses, the kind that covered the eyes entirely even at the corners.

She couldn't tell what his expression was, though he sounded cool.

"I couldn't think of any other way," she said. "I want to talk to you."

"The more we talk, the further in we get."

"There are some things I've got to tell you. If I don't, Luisa or someone else will, and I'd rather tell you myself so you'll hear it straight."

"What if I don't want to listen?"

"You've got to, Mark," she said helplessly. "You've got to."

He took off his glasses and rubbed his eyes as if they hurt. "Why don't you leave me alone?"

"I'll be gone tomorrow. Then you can forget about me."

"Christ," he said, and got out of the jeep and came around to her side. "All right. Talk. Tell me."

"Here, like this? Can't we even go somewhere and sit down? Look — we could walk over there." She pointed south, to a field of wild mustard, blazing with yellow blooms. "Isn't it pretty, Mark?"

"I guess."

"Oh, it *is* pretty. I wonder who decides which are weeds and which are flowers. Did you ever see the wild morning glories growing by the shed? They look so delicate, it's rather a shock when you find out how deep and tough their roots are."

"Is that what you wanted to tell me about, weeds?"

"Give me time."

They crossed the road, side by side, but a yard apart. The field of wild mustard wasn't fenced. The blooms came up to their knees.

"It's not a very good place to sit," he said. "There are too many bees."

"Don't you like bees?"

"Not especially."

"They don't sting unless they're frightened."

"So I've heard." He had the same feeling that he'd experienced yesterday on the boat, that everything she said was meant to have personal and philosophic implications. Her conversational asides (the dugong and its child, the storm a thousand miles away, the old man who'd planted the trees) — these were not merely observations. They were analogies, perhaps unconscious, perhaps deliberate. And now there were more of them, the bees that wouldn't sting unless they were disturbed, and the delicate morning glories with the tough roots. After only three days, even the weather wore her monogram.

He stamped down the mustard with his

feet until there was a space big enough for them both to sit down. On a hillside half a mile away, two horses were grazing.

"You don't have to tell me anything," he said, watching the horses on the scarred hill. "Someone beat you to it by half an hour."

"Who?"

"Evelyn."

"What did she tell you?"

"The straight stuff, I suppose. You had a mentally defective son, and your husband apparently killed himself."

"Why — why *apparently?*"

"It was never proved, was it? He could even have been murdered."

"But there was no one to murder him."

"Not even you?"

"Why," she whispered, "why do you say such things to me?"

"They're what I'm thinking."

She covered her face with her hands. "Such ugly things. You've got no right."

"The whole business is ugly, including the way you've tried to cover up, lie, bribe."

"I had nothing to cover up. Only my pride."

"Janet . . ."

"That first night, the way you looked at me — as if I was a real woman, not just the mother of an idiot, the widow of a suicide. I couldn't bear to have you find out. But you wouldn't understand. You're too hard to feel any pity."

"Am I?" he said bleakly.

"You have no heart. You must always figure things out, put them into words."

"They have to be put into words. Janet, why did he kill himself?"

She didn't raise her head. He pulled her hands gently away from her face so that she couldn't hide, she had to look at him.

"Why?" he repeated.

"I don't know. He was tired, I guess. You know that deep and terrible tiredness that carries on day after day as if you've never been to bed. . . ."

"Janet! For God's sake don't romanticize it. 'That deep and terrible tiredness' — that sounds fine, but what in hell does it mean? Come off it. We're talking about a man now, a real human being. You insult his intelligence, and mine too, by this pretty violin obbligato about tiredness. Other people get tired. When they do, they yawn, turn off the lights and go to bed. Oh, Christ, what's the use of talking to you?"

"Don't talk then, Mark."

"You're like all the other romantics, the Shelleyans, the members of the 'How wonderful is Death, Death and his brother

Sleep' school. I don't care whose brother Death is. I only know it's something to be avoided as long as possible, not something to dress up fancy and fall in love with, the way you've done. It's an obsession with you, totally unrelated to fact or observation. Now try again, Janet. Why did he kill himself?"

"I told you. . . ."

"Sure. He was tired."

"You're so cruel. Why do you want to hurt me?"

"I don't." A cruising bee grazed his cheek and he slapped at it impatiently. "I'm trying to save myself."

"What from?"

"You. The branding iron."

"I hate it when you talk like that. It's untrue."

He looked angry, but in a kind of melancholy way, as if the anger was only a surface substitute for another emotion. "Your memory's short. Don't you remember what you said to me this morning — that you'd rather kill me than go away from here and leave me with my family?"

"I didn't really mean it."

"Didn't you? It fits in nicely. You'd like to see me dead. Not a mangled corpse, of course. That might cramp your obsession.

But something neatly preserved, like the starfish you fixed for Jessie yesterday. You'd have a whale of a time in Madame Tussaud's, Janet. All the pretty corpses with wax guts and wax blood."

An airplane flew overhead, a swift silver fish in the sea of sky.

"I thought you *liked* me," she said, incredulous. "I didn't know you were thinking such terrible things about me. I wouldn't have come here. I wouldn't have —" *thrown the stone that killed the gander, dead under the eucalyptus tree.*

He said with an ugly smile, "Tell me, how did he kill himself?"

"He fell over the cliff."

"He flung himself over, you mean?"

"I don't know which. I wasn't there. How could I know? He just went out one night and didn't come back."

"Didn't you suspect his intention?"

"I — yes. He had tried once before."

"What did you do about it?"

"Nothing. There wasn't anything I could do."

"Maybe you didn't want to." He was appalled by his own sadism, but he couldn't hold the words back. They were a defense, his only defense against the knowledge that he had fallen in love with her. "Tell me, what was your reaction when you found out he was dead? That he was better off, out of this cold cruel world? How many euphemisms occurred to your Shelleyan mind?"

"Stop it," she cried. "You've got no right to mock me like this, and pry into my affairs."

"I have a right to know what happened to your husband, and why. You gave it to me by nominating me to take his place."

"You make everything sound dirty and cheap."

"I have to. You've been gorging yourself on euphemisms so long, you need an emetic. The main trouble with euphemism is that it's habit-forming. You get so accustomed to disguising things that you lose track of what's under which disguise."

"I don't understand some of the things you're saying. I only know you hate me — you hate me . . ."

She flung herself down in the weeds, beating the ground with her fists.

"Janet, stop. You'll hurt yourself."

"I don't care!"

He reached over and held her wrists together. "Stop now. Everything's all right."

With a little cry she turned and pressed her mouth against the back of his hand. "Mark — say you didn't mean any of it."

"I didn't mean any of it."

"I've never loved anyone before like this."

"Don't talk, darling."

The wind had risen, and the wild mustard bobbed and curtsied as it passed. In the east, beyond the hill where the two horses were grazing, a bank of clouds had formed.

Her hair, blowing against his cheek, smelled of sun and brine.

"Everything looks beautiful to me now," she said. "Does it to you too, Mark?"

"Even the ants?" he said, brushing one from her temple.

"Even the ants. Everything."

She had taken off her shoes. Her feet were large but perfect, the skin smooth all over, as if it had never felt the pressure of a shoe.

He spanned her ankle with one hand. "You have big feet."

"Haven't I though? Swimmer's feet."

"You like the water, don't you?"

"Especially the sea. Do you know, I never saw the sea until I was grown-up, and yet, when I saw it for the first time, I felt that I must have been born beside it. I recognized it — isn't that odd? — I recognized it the way people sometimes recognize a house they lived in when they were children. It was more than recognition, though. I felt a sense of destiny. I remember thinking, *here is my fate, here is the explanation, this is where I was born.*"

The return of the amphibians, he thought again, the inverse evolution, the slow way to extinction. He said, "You're a throwback, Janet. A mutation. What does the sea explain to you?"

"Everything," she said. "Everything but love. The whole hideous and intricate scheme of life and death is in the sea, but not love."

He glanced down at her and thought, fleetingly, that there was some wild justice in the fact that she had borne a child who was a mutation. He wondered how many Billys would follow the atomic war. The bomb had heralded the era of outrage, and perhaps the whole human race had already started its slow migration back to the sea. She was, then, not a throwback but a forerunner, carrying in her womb the maculate egg, the imperfect gene that doomed the world.

She sensed his withdrawal, and tried to call him back. "Don't start thinking again, will you? Don't start trying to talk me out of your life. I'm in it. You can't evict me with words." She clung to his arm, as if he had made an almost imperceptible motion to rise and walk away. "I'll tell you everything,

Mark, everything you want to know about me. After what's happened I couldn't have any secrets from you. I want to open my whole life to you."

"Better not. You feel a little submissive now, but it won't last." He took her hand, and closing the fingers one by one, made it into a fist. "Hang onto your secrets. Keep them all cosy in here for another twenty-four hours and you'll be safe. Maybe no one else will ever come so close to figuring you out."

"You're awfully vain."

"You intend to destroy me," he said. "I couldn't be more certain of it if you had a gun in your hand."

"Why don't you run away, then?"

"I can't. I'm stuck, like the remora, the fish that lives by attaching itself to the belly of a shark. You like analogies. How do you like that one?"

"It's very interesting."

"I think so, too. The remora is, naturally, safe from the shark as long as it's attached to the belly. On the other hand the shark isn't always safe from the remora because fishermen use it sometimes for bait. They tie up the remora alive, and throw it overboard, and off it goes looking for a shark's belly. In spite of its small size the remora applies enough suction to pull in the shark." He added, "We published a book on fishing once. That's the only thing I remember about it, because it made me wonder how you go about catching a live and unattached remora. Have you any ideas on the subject?"

"No."

"You might ask the sea for an explanation."

"Damn your irony," she said, "and your two-bit horoscopes. Damn everything about you!"

"With one slight exception which shall remain unnamed?"

"Damn you, damn you." She hid her face against his shoulder, weeping. But the tears came only from her eyes, they did not moisten her dry heart.

He made no attempt to comfort her. When she finally raised her head she saw that he wasn't even looking at her. He was watching the horses on the hillside. Excited by the rising wind, they raced downhill and kicked up dust.

Turning, he saw her resentment.

"I like horses," he said. "Don't you? Not in the third-at-Pimlico sense, simply to look at."

"I don't want to discuss horses."

"Very well. Anything you say."

She knew that he was ready to leave. Leaning against his arm she could feel its tenseness.

"Mark, don't go yet. Please."

"I have to. There are a few amenities to be observed. I said I was going into town for a haircut. It was the truth, too. I didn't expect to see you."

"Are you glad now that you did? You're glad I came?"

"Glad! Christ!"

"You're sorry then."

"Both," he said. "A bushel of both."

"Mark. Darling. I'll see you again, won't I? Promise me. Say it."

He shook his head, looking bleakly out toward the sea. "I don't know."

She sat where she was, in the trampled weeds, until she heard the jeep go down the road. Then slowly she began putting on her shoes.

The horses had gone back to the top of the hill again. She thought about Mark, and about the man who owned the horses. He was a deputy-sheriff named Bracken, and she had first met him a year ago, the night John was found at the bottom of the cliff.

17

He had tried twice. The first time he wrote a note and left it on the drawing board in his study along with the key to his safe deposit box and a copy of his will:

"Janet, I can't think of any other way but this. Don't blame yourself. I've been getting more and more confused lately. Please destroy this, and notify Roy Standish who will handle everything for you.

John."

He went down the stairs and outside. The night was quiet. The sea roar was muted to a whisper, and even the inexhaustible mockingbirds had been silenced.

He didn't know what time it was, except that it was after midnight and everyone was asleep. He had always had a strong sense of time; it was one of his vanities that Janet encouraged . . . *"No, I won't need my watch with John along."* . . . *"It's wonderful how John can just look at the sun and tell. . . ."*

Tonight there was no sun, and the moon cruised behind clouds. He didn't care about the time anyway. He was stepping beyond it, out of its reach, eluding the innocent trap of the hours.

The air was cold and he was wearing only his pajamas and slippers. He had been lying in bed, not actually thinking about dying at all. He had turned from his right side to his left side and back again perhaps ten times before he thought what a relief it would be not to wake up in the morning. He felt quite sorry while he was writing the note to Janet, sorry in a detached way for the poor foolish fellow who signed his name John, and who had to take such drastic measures because he wasn't strong enough to compromise.

Poor John, he thought. *Poor fellow. It can't be helped, though.*

He crossed the driveway carrying a flashlight but it wasn't necessary to turn it on yet. His eyes — all his senses — seemed to be alerted, sharpened. Even without his glasses he saw distinctly the golden discs of marigolds beside the garage, and the bristly red pompoms of the castor bean bush. The smell of kelp was overpowering, and to his ears the sound of his feet on gravel was explosive. The pebbles jumped like corn popping.

Though he had made no plans, everything worked out perfectly at the beginning. The garage door was unlocked and slid open without a squeak. The old garden hose was coiled on a nail on the wall. The ceiling light, which had burned out a week ago, had been replaced, and Janet's keys were in the ignition of the Lincoln.

He cut off a long piece of hose with a hedge clipper, and got down on his back under the rear of the car with the hose lying across his belly like an affectionate snake. He turned on the flashlight and saw that the hose was too narrow to fit over the exhaust pipe. He lay there for quite a while, wondering what he could use to bind the hose and pipe together.

It was rather pleasant lying under the car, smelling the oil and dust and gas, and looking up at the intricate mass of steel, the insides of the sleeping giant. He thought of starting the engine, leaving the throttle open a little, and then coming back to the rear of the car and breathing in the exhaust fumes, holding his mouth right up against the pipe like a child suckling. It would be very quick that way, but he somehow didn't like the idea of being found on the floor, like a victim. He preferred to be found in the driver's seat, so that people (except Janet, of course, and Roy

Standish, his lawyer) might think his death was an accident, that the wind had blown the garage door shut before he'd had a chance to drive the car out. That was silly, though. The door was too heavy to be blown shut, and anyway he was in his pajamas.

He regretted not having stopped to put on his clothes, but if he had taken that extra time he might have lost his nerve. Though he was stepping beyond the reach of time, he hadn't yet taken the final step. It was still important, he realized. Time to think, to wonder about his destination and speculate on turning back or taking a detour.

He got up again, and tossed the piece of hose into a corner. It fell against an open carton of snail bait. The carton tipped over, and some of the little pellets of poison rattled out on the cement floor. He picked them up and put them back in the carton, and then he hid the carton on a high ledge behind a can of paint, wondering who had been so careless as to leave it out in the open like that, with Billy around. *The stuff's poison,* he thought, and wiped his hands carefully on the front of his pajama top.

He closed the garage door. Climbing in behind the wheel of the Lincoln he turned on the ignition and opened the throttle a quarter of the way.

But the car hadn't been used for a week; the engine was cold and damp. He had to press the starter half a dozen times before the engine turned over with a blast of noise.

He took a deep breath and waited. The sweat of fear erupted on his face like blisters that burst and trickled coldly down his temples.

He tried not to think about himself or Janet. He began to concentrate on the chemical changes that were taking place in the air. He'd forgotten most of his elementary chemistry, but it seemed reasonable to suppose that the carbon monoxide coming from the exhaust pipe was using up the supply of oxygen in the garage and turning into carbon dioxide. When there was no more oxygen left, the carbon monoxide would remain relatively pure, and it was this pure stuff that was deadly to breathe. Or maybe this was all wrong. Maybe it didn't happen like that at all. It was too late now to find out. He breathed, in and out, his eyes blank, impassive.

There was a rush of air. In the rear mirror he saw the garage door swinging open, and in the opening stood Mr. Roma in his old paisley bathrobe.

He had time to switch off the ignition before he slumped sideways in a faint.

Other than a profound regret at his failure, and a slight red flush on the skin of his face and arms, he suffered no after effects.

Everyone was determinedly cheerful, though behind Miss Lewis's professional smile there was shock, and in Janet's eyes, reproach and bewilderment. Every minute of the day and night he was under surveillance. He couldn't take a walk along the beach without Mr. Roma suddenly finding it necessary to gather driftwood or dig for clams; and at night Janet sat up until she couldn't hold her eyes open any more. When he went to bed he closed the door of his room, but in the morning it was always open again. They kept Billy out of his way and they didn't talk about him unless he asked for information.

Later in the week Janet drove him into Marsalupe to see a doctor. The doctor gave him a dozen phenobarbital tablets and told him to cut down on his smoking and eat plenty of leafy green vegetables.

"Brilliant man," he said, on the way home.

"Who? The doctor?"

"Positively brilliant."

"Well, but you *don't* eat enough greens."

232

When they got home he flushed the tablets down the toilet. There weren't enough of them anyway, to be fatal.

It was harder to dispose of the leafy green vegetables. They appeared at the table in all forms and guises, and he ate them to please Janet.

She had wonderful control during those days. She didn't once mention the episode in the garage. No questions were asked, and no controversial matters about the future were brought up.

Every now and then he caught her looking at him in a half-hopeful, half-puzzled way. *Poor Janet,* he thought. *She's waiting for the vegetables to take effect. She can't believe it was really me who wanted to die — it was only the vitamin-deficiency.*

He felt terribly sorry for her, but he couldn't reach out to her through the strange detachment that enveloped him like a fog. She felt the fog and tried to penetrate it by talking of incidents and people from their shared past, playing the game of *Remember?*

"Remember that couple we met on the boat coming from Panama, the ones who sat and played gin rummy in the bar all day?" "It was funny, that time I got the measles and you kept saying it was only from eating too many strawberries. . . ." "I wonder what ever happened to Nancy Howard. Remember? She wanted to go on the stage but she had that awful voice. . . ."

Of course he remembered. He remembered everything. Each new day people with lost names and faces, forgotten people saying and doing forgotten things, stepped back into his memory. He seemed to have total recall, as if his mind, cleared of the future, had given the extra space to the past. His memories were vivid, but without nostalgia, without even self-pity.

A week later he had a birthday, his forty-ninth. Janet's gift to him was a new pair of binoculars she had ordered from Hammacher Schlemmer in New York.

"Thank you, Janet. It was very thoughtful of you. I needed a new pair of binoculars."

He carried them to the edge of the cliff and held them to his eyes. They were very good binoculars, but the sea was endless, the sky infinite; there was nothing to see.

At dinner he ate a piece of birthday cake and afterwards he went upstairs to say good night to Billy. It had been nearly two weeks since he'd seen him, except at a distance, walking with Miss Lewis.

Billy was sitting up in bed playing with a rubber doll that squeaked when it was pressed.

"Good night, Billy. Good night, Old Timer."

Over the railing of the bed the child looked at him as if he'd never seen him before.

"My goodness, Billy," Miss Lewis said, "don't you remember your daddy? This is your daddy. Say it now, say daddy."

Billy squeaked the rubber doll.

"Children forget easily," Miss Lewis said.

"Of course."

"Out of sight, out of mind, that's how it goes."

He took one last look at Billy and thought, *My son, my freak, my jailer. Good-bye, good-bye, poor baby.*

Janet was waiting for him downstairs. She had built a fire in the grate with monkey-puzzle boughs and the living room was subtly fragrant.

"Was he glad to see you?" Janet said.

"Oh, yes. Very."

"Can I get you anything, John?"

"No, thanks. I thought perhaps I'd go out for a short walk."

She rose immediately. "I'll go with you."

"Not this time." He went over and took her in his arms and stroked her hair gently. "Not this time, Janet," he said, staring over her head at the night that pressed against

235

the window. "You're tired. Sit here and rest for awhile."

"Promise you won't be long, then."

"It's my birthday. I'm not making any promises."

"John . . ."

"Yes?"

"When you come back we'll discuss things. We'll come to some kind of decision."

"All right."

"I *know* we can work things out between us."

"Of course."

"Perhaps we can go away on a holiday, just you and I. Wouldn't that be nice?"

"Very nice."

Turning away, he took off his glasses and put them on the mantel.

"If you're going for a walk," she said, "you'd better wear your glasses."

He remembered the night he'd gone out to the garage how alert his senses had been, how clearly he had seen the bright discs of marigolds and the red blossoms of the castor bean bush.

"I can see better without them at night."

"Then there must be something the matter. You'll have to get a new prescription."

"Tomorrow."

Perhaps it was a mistake anyway to see too clearly. Through the binoculars the sky had warned him of infinity. To the giant telescopic eye on Mount Wilson the constellations were more remotely mysterious than they were to the curious but uncritical eyes of a child. The final mystery lay not in the vastness of the stars but in the infinitesimal atoms of the mind of man.

He looked at Janet — her face was a little blurred now — and then back at the window again. Below the black horizon was tomorrow, but he felt no regret that he wouldn't be there to see it. He already knew its size and shape. *We'll talk things over, come to a decision, work things out, take a holiday.* It was all rather funny, like the doctor's advice about eating leafy green vegetables

"Janet," he said, "Janet, thanks very much for the binoculars. I really appreciated them."

He was sure she hadn't caught the error in tense, and yet there was something queer in the way she was looking at him.

"What are you staring at?" he said.

"Nothing. Let me mix you a drink before you leave."

"No, thanks."

"Promise me you won't be long?"

"No promises on my birthday, remember."

He thought that at the last moment she would follow him out, but she just sat down again in front of the fire. She watched the flames, her chin resting on her hands. Her face was nebulous, he couldn't read it without his glasses, or the binoculars, or the giant telescope.

He went outside by the back door, and passed the garage. The door had a new padlock, and the spark plugs had been taken out of the jeep and the Lincoln. He had seen Mr. Roma taking them out and Mr. Roma had seen him seeing, but they were both too polite to discuss the matter.

It was high tide. Walking along the edge of the cliff he could hear the hiss of spray and see the white uneven curves of the breakers along the shore.

He took out his watch and looked at the time on the luminous dial. It was nearly nine o'clock.

I'll wait until it's exactly nine, he thought.

He stood there until the minute hand mounted the dial and started its descent, but still he couldn't jump.

Holding the watch in his hand he walked on, blinded by the dark and his own tears.

At ten-thirty they began searching for him, Miss Lewis with the flashlight and Mr. Roma and Mrs. Wakefield carrying the two lanterns that had hung unused in the shed for years.

The lights flickered weirdly through the woods and along the barranca and the edge of the cliff. The birds, startled out of their sleep, squawked distress calls from the uncertain shelter of the leaves. The sound of the surf was like a heavy wind blowing through a forest, pausing, returning.

All this fuss, Miss Lewis thought. *There's fussing about something around here all the time. I'd like a long quiet rest in the city.*

But she raised her voice with the others, and called, "Mr. Wakefield, Mr. Wakefield . . ."

Their voices were feeble against the surf, and their lanterns helpless against the night, no better than glow worms.

"He may be walking on the beach," Miss Lewis said.

"The tide's still in," Mrs. Wakefield said. She was shivering, and her arm ached from the weight of the lantern. "There's no place to walk."

"I will look anyway," Mr. Roma said. "If you will go back to the house, I will look personally, when the tide goes out a little."

"I'm afraid."

"I know, I know."

"He's dead, I feel it."

"Go back to the house sensibly and have some coffee, something to warm you."

"Coffee sounds wonderful," Miss Lewis said in the bright firm voice she used on Billy. "Come along."

Mr. Roma set out along the cliff toward the stone steps. When he had nearly reached the bottom, just out of reach of the waves, he sat down with the lantern beside him and waited wearily until the tide went out.

Picking up the lantern he stepped down into the damp sand. Water crept into the top of his shoes and as he walked his feet made a squishing noise that increased his uneasiness; it sounded as though someone was walking behind him. He drew his coat closer, against the insinuating wind that seemed to be coming from all directions and slid up his sleeves and down his collar and up the soggy legs of his trousers.

He moved ahead slowly and cautiously. After each tide the beach changed; things were added and things were taken away. You could never walk along it as you walked on a path through the woods with the certainty that it was the same now as it was yesterday. There were always changes. A boulder had been shifted, a stranded stingray flopped in a tangle of kelp. The tide, heavier than normal, had swept away a foot of sand, exposing hundreds of fist-sized stones.

He paused for a minute, trying to decide whether to ease the stingray back into the water, or to kill and bury it so that no one would get cut by its barbed tail. As he leaned over to free it from the kelp he saw Mr. Wakefield crushed between two boulders, limp and boneless as a sponge, oozing water.

The deputy sheriff, Bracken, came in the middle of the night, and again the next day, and the next.

Bracken was a barrel-shaped man who wore a ten-gallon hat and Western boots. He had started out as a man of ideals. But as the gap increased between his ideals and the facts, he found himself owning a ranch almost paid for by contributions from the Mexican aliens who'd been smuggled into Marsalupe. They arrived by plane, they swam in from freighters, they came in false-bottomed trucks and bales of hay, and in other ways so diverse and ingenious they surprised even Bracken. The aliens didn't want to be picked up by the Immigration officers and sent back to Mexico, and Bracken didn't want to help pick them up, as long as they behaved themselves and laid off greasing their knives. After he'd had a few drinks Bracken got very sad thinking of what a hell of a fine fellow he'd been once, before those damn jigaboos came pouring into town.

He knew Mrs. Wakefield by sight. She had never spoken to him or even nodded at him, and Bracken was sensitive to slights. He thought it was a wonderful opportunity to let her know she was no better than he was, no matter where her money came from.

"Funny thing," he said, "us being neighbors all this time and never getting together for a powwow until this tragic occurrence."

She sat in silence, rubbing the knuckles on her left hand and wondering why this terrible man kept coming back to ask her the same questions over and over.

"I've told you everything I could," she said finally.

"Sure, sure, you have. We got to have an inquest, though. It's the law. You don't want to break the law, do you?"

"Naturally not. But all this endless prying into my husband's affairs . . . He's dead. What difference does it make whether it was accidental or intentional?"

"The law says we got to find out. I got to collect evidence, see what I mean?"

"Surely you've collected enough evidence already." *Enough evidence,* she thought, *and*

242

beer and coffee and ham sandwiches and any-thing else you could cram into your fat mouth.

Billy came to the door to stare at the man with the funny shoes.

Bracken said, "Get rid of the kid, will you? He gives me the heebie jeebies. I can't think."

It was that same day that the curiosity-seekers began to arrive from town. They came up the driveway in cars and along the beach on foot, pretending they were col-lecting shells or gathering mussels or looking at the view. They took away, as sou-venirs, Mr. Roma's No Trespassing signs and boughs of jacaranda and pieces of stone from the beach.

Though Billy was kept in the house, he could see the people from the windows and he sensed the excitement. The terrible and mysterious excitement made his legs tremble and brought quick tears to his eyes. No one could explain it to him, and no one tried. He was isolated in bewilderment. It was the same house he'd always known, only it was changed, like the beach after a tide.

On the morning of the inquest he was left alone with Carmelita. He sat on her lap for a long time while she rocked back and forth in her chair by the kitchen window. They were both quiet.

★ ★ ★

In the courtroom, under the drab light of the fly-specked chandeliers, a verdict of suicide was returned.

Before she had time to get away, Bracken came over and told her what a real pleasure it had been meeting her.

"Only one thing bothers me, Mrs. Wakefield. It's about that there watch of his that's still missing."

"I know nothing about it except what I've told you. He had it with him when he went out that night. He liked to — he was very conscious of time."

"Brainy guy, oh?"

She looked at him with hatred. "Oh, yes, very brainy."

"Some of these brainy ones go off their rocker just like that." He snapped his fingers; the nails were bitten to the quick. "Well, if the watch turns up, let me know. I'm a curious guy. Facts, that's what I like."

"I see."

"Well, it's been real nice meeting you anyhow. Now we've broke the ice, like they say, how about me coming over and . . ."

She turned and walked away.

She never saw Bracken again. Four days later she drove away in the Lincoln with Billy and Miss Lewis.

Looking now at the horses on the hillside that belonged to Bracken, she wondered what he would say if she phoned him and told him that the watch had been found: Yes, on the side of the cliff, Mr. Bracken, by a little girl who is as curious as you are. How did it get there, in a cormorants' ledge? I have no facts to satisfy you, Mr. Bracken. But he must have had the watch in his hand when he was standing at the top of the cliff. I've told you how he was always checking the time, looking at the minute hand on his watch, marking off the days on the calendar. Well, time was ending for him. He threw the watch as he fell, he threw it away from him, perhaps he was sick of time. . . . Quite a brainy guy, Mr. Bracken.

But the words would never be spoken. She could no longer feel any real anger at Bracken's boorish stupidity. *We are all victims,* she thought, *of ourselves and of each other. Bracken, John, Billy, myself, and now Mark, whom I love.*

She rose, turning her eyes to the sky, and thought how foolish they must all look in the eyes of heaven, how foolish and impotent and grubby, not fit to live.

18

She returned through the woods, walking very slowly, with her arms folded across her breasts. Her eyes were still swollen with tears and her cheeks stung, as if she had bathed her face in the old well that had gone to salt, thinking the water would refresh her and finding out too late that it was sharp as acid.

She passed the swimming pool that she had boarded up herself, nailing it down like a coffin, without anyone even knowing about it except Mr. Roma who had helped her fetch the planks. ("A tarpaulin would be just as good," Mr. Roma had said. "He couldn't fall in then." "No, no. It must be boarded. I had a dream, I dreamt he fell ...") What was under the planks now? What strange dark-loving creatures lived in the concrete coffin and crept through the dust and the leaves powdered by time?

At the end of one of the planks a black furry spider was spinning his web, oblivious to the wind, crossing and recrossing the silken strands with his humped legs. His old web was near by, spangled with the remains of flies. She stopped to touch the spider. It curled up into a ball from fright. She drew her hand away and walked on.

On the other side of the barranca she saw Jessie and Mr. Roma coming along the path. She knew what they were looking for even before she heard Jessie calling, "James, here James, come on home!" Stepping out of sight for a moment behind a tree, she made a futile attempt to straighten her hair and to brush from her skirt the leaves and twigs that clung to it like guilt.

"James, here James!"

"He isn't here," Mrs. Wakefield said.

"We've been looking for him everywhere. He might be lost, so we're leaving a trail of corn." Jessie's hands, and the pockets of her blue jeans were filled with kernels of corn, and Mr. Roma was carrying a paper bag.

Mr. Roma was faintly apologetic. "He likes corn, and we thought, just in case . . ."

"That's a very good idea," Mrs. Wakefield said brightly to Jessie. "You mustn't forget to leave a trail through the barranca."

"I won't."

"Can you do it all by yourself while I talk to Mr. Roma for a minute?"

"I'm not a baby!"

"I'll wait for you here then."

"All right."

With the corn dribbling out of her hand Jessie slid down the side of the barranca.

"He may be hiding," Mr. Roma said. "Like Billy."

"Like Billy, yes."

"James doesn't like the wind, he gets frightened."

"He won't be frightened this time."

"He always is. Always when there is a wind or before a storm . . ."

"Not any more." She reached out and touched the sleeve of his plaid shirt. "Mr. Roma, listen to me. I couldn't tell you in front of the child, but James is all right. He's perfectly safe."

"You know where he is?"

"Yes. Yes, and he's all right. He's better off this way, really *much* better off."

Mr. Roma bent his head. He saw the golden trail of corn winding in and out of the trees, and he heard Jessie still calling the gander, "James, James."

"What have you done?" he said heavily.

"He was so old and helpless and half-blind — I put him out of his misery."

"No, no, he was not helpless. He was not in misery."

"It was only a matter of time anyway. I found him wandering here in the woods, lost."

"He never went into the woods." Mr. Roma pressed his palms together, and she thought suddenly how grotesque his hands were, with the brown leathery skin covering the tops like half-gloves, and the undersides as pink as Jessie's cheeks. "Never further than the garage, Mrs. Wakefield. I only came out here to please the little one. I knew James never went into the woods."

"He did. Why do you keep arguing like this? Don't you believe me?"

He stood in silence with his head bowed. Beads of sweat glittered on his forehead and along his temples like tears.

"Getting emotional over a gander," she said bitterly. "Have you nothing better to cry about? We should have fattened him up years ago and put him in a roasting-pan. Don't you see that?" He didn't answer; his mouth moved, but formed no words that could be spoken. "Carl, listen. I cried today, too. Do you want to hear about it? It doesn't matter now who knows."

He seemed not to have heard. "Helpless and in misery, no, he was not. One eye, one eye was all he had, but it was all he needed." He raised his head and looked at her, and she saw in his eyes no tears, only a dry terrible grief that seemed to be not for the gander but for her.

"Don't look like that. What have *I* done?"

"Like Billy," he said.

"What?"

"Out of his misery."

"You keep talking about Billy. I don't . . ."

"The little fellow trusted you. And you — you . . ." He couldn't go on. He moved his head back and forth in helpless anger.

"I see now what's in your mind. You think I deliberately left Billy alone on deck, that I was deliberately negligent."

"You — never left him alone before."

"I've told you how it happened. He was thirsty. I went to get him a glass of water. When I left him he was playing with one of those leather-covered dolls, flinging it up in the air and trying to catch it. They found the doll afterwards, floating around in the water. They actually fished it out and gave it to me. Thoughtful, wasn't it? I was very polite. I said, thank you, thank you, good people. When it was dark I threw it overboard again. *I'm* the victim, don't you see? *I'm* the one who's suffered, not Billy, not a useless old gander . . ."

She turned her gaze toward the sea. Through an open space between trees she could see, dimly, part of the island, a little barren mountain rising out of the sea, where no one lived but a flock of sheep starving in

250

the drought, and the black vicious ravens grown fat on sheep's entrails.

"I couldn't stand it any more. Everywhere I went people stared and whispered, and then turned away breaking into self-conscious chatter. They never looked at me as if I were a person. To them I was the mother of that half-wit, the woman with the queer little boy. I was ashamed, yes, I admit it. Who wouldn't have been ashamed? Then when I came back here I met Mark and he looked at me as if I was a woman, a real woman. And I felt like one, too, for the first time in years. I've been cheated. Perhaps it's made a monster of me, I don't know. I feel that from now on I'm entitled to anything I can lay my hands on."

"My Luisa has been cheated too — to be born half-mulatto, half-Mexican — but if she talked like you I would be worried. I would wonder about her — her mind."

"Don't worry about my mind. It's very clear. I'm not muddled any more at all."

"What will you do? He — I'm sure he will not leave his family. He belongs to them."

"Only half," she said, softly. "He'll never really belong to them. And Jessie — Jessie is all mine."

"It is bad to talk like that."

"You must try to understand me, Mr.

Roma. After all, we've known each other a long time, and you've always admired me, haven't you? You've always said I was a fine woman. Those were your very words."

"Yes."

"We'll have a pleasant good-bye, then?"

"Yes, Mrs. Wakefield."

They shook hands, but at her touch he seemed suddenly to grow smaller, like the spider that had curled up into a ball from fright.

At the bend in the path he began to run. She watched him through the trees, controlling an impulse to follow him and try further to explain herself, starting right at the beginning: *I was born on a farm in Nebraska. It was scraggly little farm. I hated it. I was always terribly ambitious. I wanted to make something of myself....*

Like that, very simple and logical. But Mr. Roma had run away from her, like John, and like Mark. There was no one left to explain things to, only the deaf trees and the blithe lizards, the selfish chattering birds and the rocks worn smooth by the storms of other years.

She wheeled suddenly and called out, "Jessie? Where are you, Jessie?"

"Here."

"I can't see you."

"Right here." The top of Jessie's head, and

then the rest of her, appeared at the edge of the barranca. There were leaves caught in her yellow hair, and little spikes of twitch grass had pricked the front of her jersey.

"There you are," Mrs. Wakefield said. "There you are, of course. Let me brush you off, darling."

"You sound funny. Like my mother after she cries. Shivery, kind of."

"Does your mother cry?"

"Sometimes." Jessie began to pluck the twitch grass out of her jersey. "I made the trail. I hope he finds it and comes home."

"Surely he will."

"Maybe he's gone out to lay an egg some place, eh?"

"He can't because he's a gander, you know."

"I know. I just forgot for a minute."

"Perhaps he just got bored with us and went to find some other ganders and some geese to talk to."

"He'll come back, through?"

"Oh, yes. Someday." One by one she untangled the leaves from Jessie's hair, and they fluttered away in the wind like brown butterflies. "I'll come back too, some day."

Jessie's mouth gaped in surprise. "Are you going *away?*"

"Tomorrow."

"I thought you were going to *live* with us for a long time."

"No, Jessie."

Hand in hand they began walking along the path. When they came to the swing in the pepper tree they found Jessie's doll sitting on the wooden seat. The doll was nearly scalped from being carried around by the hair, but it was dressed sumptuously in a purple scarf belted with one of Mark's ties.

Jessie took the doll and flung it in the dirt. She suddenly hated it, and she didn't care if her father's tie got dirty or not.

"I could come with you," she said at last.

"No. No, Jessie, not this time."

"I wouldn't be any trouble."

"I know that, but . . . You'd better pick up your doll and clean her off. What's her name?"

"Marie. I just hate her."

"I'll send you a new doll," Mrs. Wakefield said. "The very best and biggest one I can find."

"I like the kind that wet and burp."

"Then that's the kind you'll get. What will you name her?"

"I don't know," Jessie said slowly. "I guess I don't really want a new doll anyway. I'd rather just go with you."

"Why?"

Jessie shook her head. She couldn't tell why. She only knew that with Mrs. Wakefield she felt quite independent and grown up. Mrs. Wakefield never told her to be quiet or to go and wash her hands or to stop biting her hangnail.

"If I came with you," she said, "we could catch lots of starfish and I wouldn't mind a bit about them being boiled."

"But you'd miss your father and mother."

"I could write to them."

Mrs. Wakefield had turned quite pale. "Some day — some day you'll come and visit me."

"When?"

"I don't know."

"Where?"

"I don't know that, either."

"That's the same as *never*," Jessie said harshly.

"No, dear. No, it isn't."

"It just means *never*." Never was not a word, it was a tone, a look, a gesture. "You don't want me to come visiting you."

"I do, very much. More than I can tell you." She sat down on the swing and put her arm around Jessie's shoulders. "You must be patient and so must I. We both had disappointments today. We have to face them, though. There'll be other disappointments for both of us, all kinds and shapes and sizes."

"You told me different before! You read my hand . . ."

She twisted out of Mrs. Wakefield's grasp. Giving the doll a final and decisive kick, she picked it up by the hair and dragged it along in the dirt and through the piles of sharp oak leaves.

Cramming it under a fuzzy green anise bush she felt a bitter satisfaction. It was inevitable that some day her father would question her about the tie, and that Evelyn would ask what happened to "that lovely doll your Aunt Susan gave you." But she didn't care. The doll was the symbol of the disappointment, the image both of her parents who wouldn't let her go, and of Mrs. Wakefield who wouldn't take her. It was the physical form of *never*, the *impossible* dressed in a purple scarf and a wig. Once the doll was thoroughly beaten and out of sight, her spirits began to rise a little.

She broke off a twig of anise and put it in her mouth. Mr. Roma said that anise was the favorite food of the swallow-tailed butterfly when it was a cocoon, and there was the magic possibility that if she ate enough of it she too would suddenly sprout wings and be able to fly anywhere she liked. The possibility of magic was delightful, but alarming too, because if there was good magic there would also be bad magic. Her father had told her so when he was reading aloud from Grimm's fairy tales. The system of weights and balances wasn't perfect, he said; the darker magic was heavier.

"That's not good for you," Mrs. Wakefield said, coming up behind her. "Spit it out, Jessie."

She spit it out, but the wind was against her and she had to borrow Mrs. Wakefield's handkerchief to wipe off her face.

Mrs. Wakefield shook the handkerchief and put it back in her pocket. She was still very pale, and her eyes seemed misty and remote. She looked like *never*.

"If you come with me," she said softly, "I know where we'll go."

"Where?"

"The island. See?"

Jessie looked, and there was the island, the magic island that appeared and vanished with every whim of the weather. Sometimes it was blue, and sometimes gray; or it was not there at all, or it was only a tip visible above the low fog, like a castle built on clouds.

"I was silly not to think of it before, wasn't I?" Mrs. Wakefield said, laughing. "Why, the

257

island would be a wonderful place for you and me. All the starfish we want, and other things, lots of wonderful things."

"You said no one lives there."

"Of course we can't live there just yet. But we can go and look around. We can see if we like it or not."

"When?"

"Right now. And then if we like it we can make plans."

"It looks far."

"It's too far to swim, naturally. But you and I, we'll take the boat, the rubber one because that's safer. And you can help me make it go."

Hesitating, Jessie scuffed the ground with the toe of one shoe. "I don't much like boats."

"You won't desert me too, will you, Jessie? No, of course you won't, of course not." She pressed Jessie's hand between her own two hands. "You want to see the island, don't you? Imagine a whole island all to ourselves."

"I'll have to go to school some place."

"School?" Mrs. Wakefield repeated blankly. "Oh. Yes. Such a sober little girl you are. Like Mark. always thinking. All right, all right we'll *build* a school. How's that? Now we'd better hurry."

"I've got to tell my mother. She may want me to put on a sweater or something."

"But this is a secret, Jessie. You can tell her when we get back. Or she'll be able to see for herself if she looks out of the window, that we've just gone for a little boat-ride. We must hurry, though. Listen."

Through the woods, harsh and clear, came the sound of Mr. Roma's cow-bell.

"Someone wants me," Jessie said.

"We won't pay any attention."

"Maybe my father's come home. He promised to bring me some gum."

"I'll buy you lots of gum," Mrs. Wakefield murmured, close to her ear. "And the biggest doll we can find. And the island, too. We'll build a school and a house as big as a castle." But *never*, her eyes said, and the cypress mauled by the wind dropped its dying needles and whimpered, *Never.*

Jessie didn't hear it or see it, but her skin pricked, and just under her left shoulder blade she had a little twinge of pain, sharp as a tack.

"I'm — I better go home first anyway."

"Why?"

"I don't like the wind. I just *hate* it!"

"But it's pretty. Like music. Very special music so that only special people like you and me can hear it."

Jessie listened, but she couldn't hear any music, only the rhythmic clanging of the cow-bell calling her home. She put her fingers in her ears and lowered her head against the wind.

"The wind will die down soon," Mrs. Wakefield said. "Up here on the cliff we feel it more. Come on, Jessie."

"Is there — is there *really* an island?"

"Of course, darling. You can see it for yourself."

"Sometimes not."

"It's always there."

She began to move along the path with her hand resting on Jessie's shoulder. At first Jessie didn't like her hand there — it was too heavy, it impeded her walking. But gradually it became a comfort to her, an anchor against the wind. She lengthened her stride to match Mrs. Wakefield's. There was a little barb of excitement caught in her throat; she was walking beside Mrs. Wakefield, stride for stride like a grown woman, and she was taking a trip to an island where no one lived.

They skirted the side of the house and headed for the stone steps a hundred yards beyond. No one saw them or challenged them, though they had a glimpse of Mr. Roma standing where James used to stand, under the magnolia tree. The cow-bell was silent.

"I think my father's home," Jessie said. "I saw the jeep."

"You'll see him when we come back." She began to talk fast, trying to keep Jessie's attention away from the house and the jeep parked in the driveway. "Last night I had a dream. It was funny. I dreamt the sea had dried up, and where the sea had been there was a vast hole covered with dust and crushed salt. In the hole, everything, all the fish and seals and porpoises, lay gasping and half-dead. There was no water anywhere in the world. Everything had come down to the sea to drink, birds and animals and people. Even people I know were there, Luisa and you — you were there, Jessie. But of course the sea had dried up, too. There was only this great hole."

"That's silly," Jessie said.

"Dreams are. Then it began to rain, and the sea filled up, and everything came to life like magic. There was no lightning or thunder, just the rain. I walked in it. I walked in the woods, and out of the dust grew beautiful flowers, and the path was a velvet ribbon of grass. Not just devil grass, the kind we have now — this was real grass with a little clover in it. And the trees — ah, you should have seen the trees, Jessie. The live oaks seemed to reach almost the sky.

Every orange tree was jeweled with gold, and the leaves of the peppers hung down like moist green lace. I could see things growing quite plainly. Buds opened before my eyes, and from bare wood little green sprouts emerged . . ."

"The sea was all right again, though?"

"Yes, it was all right. Just the way it is now."

"Kind of rough?"

"Yes."

"Did you swim in it?"

"No, I woke up too soon."

"That's a funny dream," Jessie said, nodding gravely. "It certainly is."

In single file they started down the stone steps holding onto the rust-blistered iron rail guard. Just before the house dipped out of sight Jessie turned to look back at it, and a secretive little smile crossed her face. She felt quite dashing and adventurous, following Mrs. Wakefield down the steps, and seeing ahead of her in the distance the island, the shape of a giant curled up on his side asleep. She wasn't in the least afraid even when she thought of the giant-image, because they had reached the bottom of the steps now and Mrs. Wakefield had taken her hand again and was holding it very securely.

"I'm glad you're coming with me," Mrs.

Wakefield said gaily. "It wouldn't be any fun visiting the island all by myself."

"What will we do when we get there?"

"Explore. Or maybe we'll watch the porpoises first."

"How do you know there are porpoises?"

"A fisherman told me. He tried to catch one with a jig, but the porpoises were too clever to be fooled. Then he found out later what bad luck it is to catch a porpoise, so he stopped trying. Fishermen are superstitious."

"Why?"

"Because they live by luck. You're not getting cold, are you?"

"No." But she was a trifle cold, in spite of the midafternoon sun. The masses of foam blowing along the beach like soapsuds had dampened her jeans, and they were beginning to feel soggy, flapping against her legs.

"Here we are, Jessie."

The rubber boat was where Mark had left it, half-pulled up on the big rock out of reach of the tide. Mr. Roma's old rowboat was there too, upside down, showing its gray slivered bottom.

Mrs. Wakefield tugged at the raft until it came bouncing down into the sand. Tautened by the sun-warmed air inside, it seemed ready to burst. But when they dragged it across the sand into the cold water it began to shrink until it was quite flabby.

"It's leaking," Jessie said, stepping back up on the dry sand.

"No, it's not. It's just the change in temperature." Mrs. Wakefield had kicked off her shoes and was standing in the water holding the raft steady against the pressure of the breakers. "Take your shoes off and roll up your jeans. I'll hold it while you get in."

Jessie obeyed, slowly. The raft, which looked so enormous when it was carried on top of the car, now looked hardly big enough for two.

"Hurry up, Jessie."

"I am. I've got a knot."

"Leave it then."

Mrs. Wakefield's dress was soaked all the way to her waist, but she didn't seem to mind. She was smiling, and when a wave broke over the raft, slapping its flabby yellow flanks, she let out an excited little laugh.

"Isn't this fun, Jessie?" she cried. "Look at me, I'm drenched! Come on now, climb in, darling."

"But it won't stay *still*."

"Of course it won't. Imagine a boat that would stay still. No one would want such a thing. Come on now."

"I'm coming."

Holding up her jeans she stepped into the water. An outgoing wave sucked at her feet and left her up to her ankles in sand. She wished that there was an easier way of getting to the island, such as a bridge or a big ferryboat that didn't bounce so sickeningly.

She wriggled over the side of the raft, and sat down, stiff with pride and fright, on the little rubber seat in the stern.

"Good girl. Now when I get in we must both paddle as hard as we can to get beyond the breakers. Can you do that?"

"I — guess so."

"All right then. *Bon voyage*, Miss Banner."

Jessie giggled, holding her hand over her mouth.

19

Carmelita had closed the drapes in the living room so the afternoon sun wouldn't fade the carpet. The room was so dark in contrast to the glare outside that Mark didn't see Evelyn until she spoke:

"Home so early?"

"Yes."

As his eyes adjusted to the gloom, he could see her more clearly, curled up on the davenport as limp as a rag doll, holding in her lap the half-finished sweater she was knitting for Jessie. The ball of yarn was way over by the fireplace as if it had been thrown there in a fit of rage.

He said carefully, "I didn't get a haircut."

"So I see."

"As a matter of fact, I didn't get to town at all. I turned around and came back. The wind was so heavy it was like trying to drive through a sand storm on the desert."

He sat down in a chair opposite her, and rubbed his knuckles against the side of his jaw. He needed a shave and a shower, but he knew that Evelyn expected him to sit down and talk. She had probably been lying there for hours planning what to say to him.

"What have you been doing all afternoon?" he asked her.

"Thinking."

"What about? Or is that the wrong question?"

"Home, mostly."

"Homesick already?"

"A little bit." She stirred, picked up her knitting and let it drop again into her lap. "I know we had a hundred reasons for coming here, but I can't remember one of them. Isn't that funny?"

"To avoid the heat," Mark said, "and to breathe the bracing sea air. Also I believe it was mentioned that travel would broaden Jessie."

"I don't feel very braced. And up to today, the heat's been practically as bad as it is in Manhattan. Do you think Jessie is being broadened?"

"Oh, yes. Definitely. We all are. It's been a liberal education."

"Don't get ironic."

"I'm not."

"You can't talk to me for three minutes any more without getting ironic. Is it — it *is* because of her, isn't it?"

"No."

"You don't lie to me often. I can always tell when you do."

"Can you?" he said wearily. "I can hardly tell myself sometimes."

He reached for the cigarette box on the coffee table in front of him. The box, as usual, was filled, the cigarettes were fresh, and the table lighter worked at the first try. Detail was Evelyn's specialty. He felt vaguely irritated that she should waste so much time on such relatively unimportant things. "Do we have to have it so gloomy in here?"

"The carpets will fade."

"They belong to Mrs. Wakefield. You don't like her anyway, why not fade her damned carpets?"

"That's a beautiful thought. I will."

She got up and flung back the drapes. Dust swirled in the shafts of sunlight.

"Please tell me the truth, Mark. It can't possibly be any worse than what I've imagined."

"There's not much truth to tell."

"She hasn't been here all afternoon. Was she with you?"

"Some of the time. We said good-bye. Permanently. She's leaving tomorrow morning, and after that I don't expect to see her again. You can stop thinking about her."

"Can I? Can *you?*" There was a ghastly little smile on her face. "Was the farewell — quite touching?"

"Yes, it was. Most farewells are."

"But this one — this one specially, eh?"

"Stop it, Evelyn." He stared into the swirling dust and wished he was a part of it, unable to feel.

"You're suffering, aren't you?" she said, her mouth shaking. "Underneath all that wonderful masculine control of yours, I can see you suffering. And I'm glad. I'm laughing, see? Now you know how other people feel, don't you? Now it's your turn, and I'm glad. I'm so glad I could die laughing!" She put up her arm and hid her face against her sleeve. "Other — other people can suffer, too."

He walked over to her and put his hands on her trembling shoulders.

"Leave me alone!"

"I just wanted to say that I'm sorry. I'm very sorry, Evelyn."

"I know you are. But I don't happen to want any tender apologies. They don't affect me any more. You're rotten spoiled, Mark. You always have been, always the little king of the castle, with all your sisters dancing attendance on you, and your parents spending half their time convincing you

you were the Great Brain. And where they left off, I took over. I became the stooge. I guess I shouldn't complain now that I'm getting what stooges usually get, a custard pie smack in the puss. Hilarious." One corner of her mouth turned up in a bitter little smile. "How am I doing in my role of the wronged wife?"

"Just fine," he said soberly. "Go on."

"I haven't anything more to say, except that you're a hard man, Mark — oh, very gentle and sweet when it comes to dogs or children or horses — but hard on people, on me, and on her too, I guess. I — I could almost sorry for her. Maybe some day I will."

"And me?"

"Oh, yes, I'll feel sorry for you, too. How can I help it when I love you?"

The cigarette had burned down to his fingers and the real physical pain of the burn was almost a relief. He opened the window to throw away the butt. The wind fussed, and swept the smoke into the corners of the room like a whining housewife. Closing the window again he saw, a quarter of a mile from shore, the yellow raft bouncing on the choppy, whitecapped waves. The raft was headed out to sea and Mrs. Wakefield was paddling with frenzied speed. In the stern, looking tiny and vulnerable, sat Jessie.

"She must be crazy!" he said incredulously.

"Who?"

"She's got Jessie out there in the raft with an offshore wind like this." He wheeled around in fury. "Where's Roma?"

"I — I sent him to call Jessie."

Mr. Roma was beside the old shed hanging up the cowbell on its nail.

He turned at the sound of Mark's feet running across the driveway.

"Jessie doesn't come. I rang and rang . . ."

"She's out in the raft with Mrs. Wakefield."

"The raft?" Mr. Roma shook his head in bewilderment. "But it's too rough, Mrs. Wakefield should know that. The small craft warnings are up all the way from Point Concepcion, I heard it on the radio."

"We'll have to go after them."

"Better to phone the Coast Guard and say urgent."

"There isn't time." He grabbed Mr. Roma's arm and shouted, "They're headed out to sea, deliberately. They're not just out joyriding. They're going some place!"

"There's no place to go. Only the island."

"That's miles away!"

"Twenty miles." The whites of Mr. Roma's eyes seemed to be swelling like bal-

271

loons. "And there's nowhere to land. Just the straight cliff, and the tide caves . . ."

"For Christ's sake!" Mark said helplessly. "For Christ's sake!"

"We'll go after them in the rowboat. Wait, and I'll get a blanket."

Seconds later he came running out of the kitchen door with two blankets over his arm, and Carmelita at his heels screaming at him in Spanish. He paid no attention.

Racing to the edge of the cliff behind Mark, he threw the blankets over. They began to climb down, half-sliding, half-falling, clutching at jutting roots and chaparral to slow their descent. Almost simultaneously they fell sprawling on the beach in a landslide of rock and earth.

Mark's hands were bleeding and there was a spot on the back of his head that was already starting to swell. "Are you all right, Roma?"

"Yes."

"The boat doesn't look too good."

"It is, though."

"We'll find out soon enough."

They eased the rowboat off the rock into the sand and carried it down to the water. Mr. Roma fitted the oars into the rusted locks.

"I'll row," he said.

"No. I'm going to."

"Better for me to do it. Your hands . . ."

"They don't bother me. Get in."

The boat lurched wildly through the breakers. Leaning forward, Mr. Roma shielded the blankets with his body to keep them dry. Except for the cut on his cheek that was bleeding slowly, his face had a mauve tinge, and his eyes still seemed ready to burst like the eyes of a fish reeled up suddenly from the vast pressure at the bottom of the sea. He didn't speak. He sat huddled over the blankets, his gaze fixed on the bottom of the boat, where the water that had splashed over the bow rolled back and forth across his boots.

"Why did she do this, Roma?"

"I — I don't know exactly."

"Maybe she doesn't realize the danger."

"She must. But she doesn't care. She told me, she said she had been cheated, that she was entitled to anything she could lay her hands on."

"What did she mean?"

Mr. Roma raised his head and looked out toward the little raft. "I guess she meant the — the child."

"What else?" Mark screamed above the wind. "Tell me what else . . ."

"She said Jessie was all hers."

"Hers?"

"I think she meant she would take Jessie away with her some place."

"But there isn't any place to take her."

"The island."

"They'd never get to the island in that thing!"

"She doesn't care," Mr. Roma said again.

There was rage and fear now behind every pull of the oars. The boat was catching up easily with the clumsy rubber raft, but neither Mrs. Wakefield nor Jessie had turned around and seen it. They seemed inexorably headed for a destination.

Mrs. Wakefield looked so funny with her hair streaming and her dress puffing in and out with the wind, that Jessie could hardly stop laughing. Wind-tears and laughter-tears squeezed out of her eyes, and dried saltily on her blotched cheeks.

"My arms are getting tired," Jessie said.

"Rest a while then. I will, too."

"Will we find seals there, do you think?"

"Certainly."

"I'd like to catch a baby one to take home with me. I bet the kids at school wouldn't believe their eyes."

"Home?" Mrs. Wakefield half-turned, so that Jessie could see how very still her face had become. Her hair blew, her dress fluttered, but her face was quiet as stone. "Where's home?"

"Manhattan."

"Manhattan." She spoke with her fingers pressed against her mouth. "That's an island too, isn't it?"

"A city-island."

Shivering, Jessie hugged her arms together to warm them. The sun had disappeared and a flock of clouds was blowing across the sky. The sea was changing color, from blue to green, and silver to slate. She was a little awed by all the changes, and she looked toward the island to see how close they were getting, and how soon they would be arriving.

But the island had vanished. There was only the sea, going on and on and on.

"It's gone," she shouted. "The island's gone!"

"No, no, it hasn't. It's still there, only we can't see it. The weather's changed."

"But we're getting closer to it. We should see it *better*. It should be *bigger*."

"It's only hiding behind the weather."

"Hiding?" She leaned forward straining her eyes, but there was nothing hiding out there. The sleeping giant had wakened, and walked away.

She remembered the mystery of the puddles on the highway. It had been a sunny day, and she was out driving with her father when she noticed on the pavement ahead of her shining wet puddles. But no matter how fast her father drove he never caught up with the puddles, they had always dried up and disappeared by the time the car reached them.

"Why can't we catch them?" she had asked.

"Because they're not there," Mark said. "It's only the reflection of the sun's rays."

"But I *see* them, I see them with my own eyes!"

"It's an illusion."

"But . . ."

"See that one right now beside the maple tree? When we get to the tree we'll stop and you can get out and look."

She got out and looked, and there was no puddle. She picked a maple leaf off the ground to take home and wax, as a souvenir.

"There isn't any island," she said in a hard tight little voice.

"Jessie, I've told you . . ."

"It's like the puddles. I looked and they weren't really there."

"I don't understand. Jessie dear, listen . . ."

She climbed over the seat and put her arms coaxingly around the resisting child.

Then she saw, not more than fifty yards behind the raft, Mr. Roma and Mark in the old rowboat. "Perhaps you're right," she said harshly. "There isn't any island."

"It was all pretend?"

"Yes."

"And we can go home?"

"Yes."

"You shouldn't play jokes like that on people," Jessie said righteously. "It isn't nice."

"I see that now."

"You won't do it any more?"

"No, Jessie. Never."

"That's a promise."

"Look. Look behind you. Your father and Mr. Roma have come to — to meet us."

"My *father!*" Jessie swung round, and there, her eyes told her, was her father, and Mr. Roma, and the rowboat. There was no island, but her father was real, and so was the rowboat, and the realest of all was Mr. Roma. He'd taken off his hat and was waving it furiously. His face was all squeezed up with smiles, and he kept nodding and shaking his head so hard it seemed that his neck had come loose.

Jessie screamed with laughter and shouted to him though he couldn't hear her: "Mr. Roma! Hey, there *isn't* any island! It's just a joke!"

Mrs. Wakefield put out the sea-anchor. She sat in silence until the rowboat pulled up alongside and Mark grabbed the rope that was tied to the sides of the raft.

"Ahoy, ahoy," Jessie yelled, and Mr. Roma yelled back, "Ahoy!"

"Hey, Mr. Roma! Do you know what? There *isn't* any island."

"Fancy that," said Mr. Roma, sniffing and wiping his eyes on his shirtsleeve. "Fancy that now."

"Daddy, did you know that?"

"No," Mark said. "Here. I'll help you over. You're going back with us."

"But why?"

"Be a good girl and don't ask questions. Step right here now, in the middle."

He held her as she clambered over the side. Mr. Roma wrapped her in a blanket like a cocoon and she sat pressed tight against his side, rocking back and forth with the motion of the boat.

Mark turned to Mrs. Wakefield, his face cold with anger. "Are you coming?"

"No."

"Pulling a crazy stunt like this — you must be out of your mind. Now get in here."

"I don't want to."

"You're going to, anyway."

"You're only wasting time," Mrs. Wakefield said. "Jessie should be taken home. Her clothes are wet."

"What are you going to do?"

"I?" She blinked. "I'll — I'll be back in a little while."

"The wind's against you, and it looks as if it's going to storm."

"We never have summer storms here."

"For Christ's sake, Janet, stop arguing. Haven't you been foolish enough for one day? I can't leave you out here like this, and I've got to get Jessie home."

"Take her then. I don't want to go back just — just yet. In a little while. I'll be there in a little while."

"Janet — Janet, please. Act sensible."

"Leave her be," said Mr. Roma, and Mrs. Wakefield looked across at him, gratefully.

"What about the storm?" Mark shouted.

"Storm? Like Mrs. Wakefield told you, we never have a summer storm."

"Thank you, Carl," she said.

It began to rain before they reached shore.

Mr. Roma said that Mrs. Wakefield had gone on a long journey, and Evelyn said she didn't know . . . *"Hush now, Jessie. No one knows. There's no use asking any more questions."*

But Luisa, whispering from her window

across the dark wet driveway, said *she* knew. "She's at the bottom of the sea. The sharks are eating her."

"No!"

"They are so, I bet."

"Mr. Roma said . . ."

"You're such a baby they don't *tell* you things. I happen to know they found the raft two days ago. The Coast Guard found it in a tide cave on the island."

"What island?"

"*The* island, silly."

"You're a stinking liar," Jessie said and closed her window tight and put her fingers in her ears so she couldn't hear the trees crying in the dark outside her window, drip, drip, drip.

It was nearly a week before the rain stopped and the sun came out and it was all right to go into the woods again.

She shuffled down the path wearing an old pair of ladies' rubber boots that Mr. Roma had found in the garage and brushed the cobwebs out of. ("Whose are they, Mr. Roma?" "No one's." "They must belong to someone." "Hush, no more questions." "Are they Mrs. — ?" "Now, now.")

It wasn't raining, but the trees still dripped when she shook their branches, or when the hummingbirds darted in and out of the wet leaves. The path had turned to mud that squished, and tugged at the oversize boots trying to pull them off. When she was out of sight of the house she reached down and picked up a handful of the mud to see how it felt; and there, already growing up out of it, was a miniature tree, with delicate lacy leaves like a pepper tree.

She stared down at it, frowning. The little tree reminded her of something, but for a moment she couldn't think what. She glanced around her more carefully and then she saw that there were other little trees too, growing all around her feet, and tiny leaves sprouting from twigs and branches that she'd thought were dead. Everything had come to life again like magic. From bare wood little green sprouts had emerged, and buds seemed to be opening right before her eyes. (*Then it began to rain, and the sea filled and everything came to life . . .*")

It was all there, just as it had been there in Mrs. Wakefield's dream. The orange trees glittered with gold, and the live oaks reached the sky, and the leaves of the peppers hung down like moist green lace.

"I bet she never had a dream," she said aloud, scornfully. "I bet she just saw it for herself and *said* it was a dream."

What a liar Mrs. Wakefield was, making up that story about the island, and what a baby she herself had been to believe it. She was much older now. No one could ever fool her again.

She walked on, crushing the little trees deliberately with the heels of her boots.

We hope you have enjoyed this Large Print book. Other Thorndike Press or Chivers Press Large Print books are available at your library or directly from the publishers.

For more information about current and upcoming titles, please call or write, without obligation, to:

Thorndike Press
P.O. Box 159
Thorndike, Maine 04986 USA
Tel. (800) 257-5157

OR

Chivers Press Limited
Windsor Bridge Road
Bath BA2 3AX
England
Tel. (0225) 335336

All our Large Print titles are designed for easy reading, and all our books are made to last.